A Kristin Ashe Mystery

If No One's
LOOKING

JENNIFER L. JORDAN

Spinsters Ink
2008

Spinsters Ink
P.O. Box 242
Midway, Florida 32343

Printed in the United States of America on acid-free paper
First Edition

Editor: Cindy Cresap
Cover designer: LA Callaghan

ISBN-10: 1-883523-87-7
ISBN-13: 978-1-883523-86-2

For those who will never belong . . .

About the Author

Jennifer L. Jordan, a two-time Lambda Literary Award Finalist, is the author of *A Safe Place To Sleep*, *Existing Solutions*, *Commitment To Die*, *Unbearable Losses*, *Disorderly Attachments* and *Selective Memory*, all mysteries in the Kristin Ashe series.

For more information or to read excerpts of her books, visit her Web site at www.JenniferLJordan.com.

Kristin Ashe Mysteries by Jennifer L. Jordan
If No One's Looking
Selective Memory
Disorderly Attachments
Unbearable Losses
Commitment To Die
Existing Solutions
A Safe Place To Sleep

PROLOGUE

I looked down and saw drops of blood.

Wiping my hand on my jeans, I continued to push through the stand of oak brush, scarcely mindful of the sharp limbs. A light drizzle had begun to fall, and lightning flashed in the distance, but neither slowed me.

Miles into my circuitous search, I'd crossed wetlands, cut through copper-colored fields of tall grass and thistle and hiked in and out of gullies. For the most part, though, I'd stayed on the hard-packed dirt trails that followed and intersected the meandering of Plum Creek.

All the while, my eyes rarely left the ground as I shifted them from left to right, and back to left again, in meticulous twenty-foot sweeps. After more than four hours, I had yet to come across another soul, and with darkness soon to fall, it seemed unlikely I would.

What a contrast this was to five days earlier . . . to the day when it seemed as if every lesbian in Denver was looking for Kayla Martin.

CHAPTER 1

"Got a good feeling about this," Fran Green said on that Sunday morning in mid-September.

I squinted and bit my lower lip. "I don't."

She nudged me on the arm. "Worried I forgot something?"

I looked around Founders Park. "That's not it."

Fran reached into her backpack and handed me a tube of sunscreen. "Lots of balls in the air. Might have overlooked a detail or two."

"I can't believe you coordinated this on such short notice," I said, squeezing out a ribbon of cream.

"Telling you, Kris, wasn't easy." Fran sighed and made a swooping gesture. "Called in every marker and then some. Be in arrears for years."

"You won't owe anyone anything. It's for a good cause."

"True enough."

"Where did all this come from?"

"All corners of Denver. Muffins and breads donated by our favorite bakery on Sixth Avenue. Fresh fruit and power bars chipped in from the organic market downtown. Bottled water and ice, compliments of our insurance agent. Hiking club brought the coolers. Hope they marked whose is whose. Always getting 'em mixed up on our outings. DJ from that new nightclub, Oblivion, brought the sound system. Also hooked me up with event planners. They hauled in the tents, tables and chairs."

I eyed the crowd that was growing by the minute. "How'd you get so many women to show up?"

"Put out a call to every group I know. Got the bikers, chorus members, softball players, golfers, bowlers. Good showing from the Metropolitan Community Church. Global positioning hobbyists, too. They'll come in handy."

"You knew someone from each of those circles?"

"Most. Otherwise, knew someone who knew someone. Thumbed through the Rolodex, then let viral marketing take over. Even got a group to come down from Cheyenne. Over there in the cowboy hats," Fran said, pointing to a cluster of women standing on concrete, under a metal pavilion. "Wish I could've made an announcement on my radio show Thursday, but word didn't come down till end-of-business Friday. Hit the phone lines hot and heavy yesterday. So amped up, didn't catch two winks of sleep last night."

"You don't look tired."

After a sleepless night, my business partner, at sixty-seven, looked more vigorous than most of the women who had gathered at the park, many of whom were decades younger than Fran. Dressed in cargo shorts, thick wool socks, 1970s-style hiking boots and a yellow T-shirt with black lettering, *Keep It Real,* Fran had covered her nose in a white cap of sunscreen. Beneath her safari hat, she wore aviator, mirrored sunglasses, and around her belt, she'd clipped a can of bear spray, a six-inch hunting knife and a fanny pack with two water bottles.

"That's just it. Don't feel tired. Not at all." Fran clicked her two walking sticks together. "Got more energy now than I had five years ago. Must be those vitamins I been taking."

"Mmm," I said as I watched an attractive, long-limbed woman with shoulder-length, blond hair climb onto a picnic table and motion for the crowd to quiet.

"Good turnout. This much manpower, bound to find something," Fran added.

"Shh."

"Could I have everyone's attention, please?" the woman in front called out. "Thank you. I'm Destiny Greaves, the executive director of the Lesbian Community Center, and on behalf of Gwen Martin and Tracey Reid, I'd like to thank you for coming on such short notice. I've never seen this degree of support and commitment from the community. Unfortunately," she said after a pause, "we need all of it. A three-year-old's life could depend on you."

Destiny held up a flier with a picture of a bright-eyed girl in a princess costume. "We're here today because Kayla Martin went missing three days ago. She was last seen around one o'clock in the afternoon, on Thursday, September thirteenth. She was in her home on South Pine Lane, which is a block east of here. At the time of her disappearance, Kayla was wearing a pink tank top with flowers, blue jean shorts and Little Mermaid underwear."

Destiny took a deep breath. "Kayla has blond hair and blue eyes, weighs thirty-five pounds and is forty inches tall. We're operating on the assumption that she was abducted from inside the house, sometime between one and four, while her mother, Tracey, was sleeping. We also have to consider that she might have wandered into the street and been picked up by a stranger. The Highlands Ranch Police Department has issued a statewide Amber alert, but no significant leads have come in."

"Who's that bombshell next to Destiny?" Fran whispered.

I shot her a look as my answer.

"That makes what we're doing today extremely important," Destiny continued. "We anticipate registering more than two hundred volunteers, which will allow us to search a sizable area. I'm going to turn this over to Lieutenant Hillary Longhorn, our liaison from the Highlands Ranch Police Department, and let her explain how we'll coordinate the search. Again, on behalf of Gwen and Tracey, thank you for your time and show of support. Both mean the world to them."

Destiny pointed toward two women who were standing off to the side of the pavilion holding hands. Both looked to be in their late twenties, and they waved limply at the crowd, their blank expressions never changing. I wondered which one was Tracey, the mother who had "lost" Kayla. Was she the tall, slightly overweight, matronly one with her hair pulled back in a ponytail, a row of bangs almost touching her eyebrows? Or the lanky one, with a grim set of her jaw and medium-length curly hair partially tucked under a baseball cap?

The police officer climbed onto the picnic bench and took the microphone from Destiny. "Folks, we all have the same goal in mind. Find Kayla as soon as possible. Today, however, we need to make our focus more narrow than that. Find anything that might tie to Kayla. The smallest clue can lead to a further development, and multiple clues can be assembled into a trail of clues. I've seen that happen before in cases, when the efforts of volunteer searchers have led straight to the doorstep of a perpetrator."

I suppressed a yawn and glanced at my watch. It was barely six o'clock, and the sun was beating down, without a cloud in sight.

"But I don't want to get your hopes up," Hillary Longhorn said in a deep voice. "Searching can be dull, tedious work, and you need to stay alert during every minute of it. If your team clears an area, that will be the last time that particular section is searched. Accuracy matters more than speed. By day's end, we hope to have canvassed fifty-five areas that we've identified as high priority, and we'll fan out from there if time permits. You'll be going block by block, step by step, focusing on the medians and edges of streets.

"We're going to ask that you mark or pick up everything you see, which means you'll be gathering trash. Lots of it. Fast food wrappers, water bottles and caps, cigarette butts, beer cans, lids, straws—you'll bag it all and bring it back here to central command. Don't rule out anything. Something that might seem commonplace could be a piece of the puzzle, and we won't necessarily know immediately which ones are relevant. We have to assume they all are. Every item will be examined and held as evidence. If you come across anything that seems particularly unusual, have your team leader mark the location with a flag and call it in. This isn't a scavenger hunt, so don't be discouraged if you don't find anything. Information that comes from elimination can be just as valuable to an investigation."

"Man, oh, man, she's hot," Fran said out of the side of her mouth. She pointed her thumb at Lieutenant Longhorn, who stood with her weight on her left foot, her right hand in the pocket of creased black slacks. Her ear-length, salt-and-pepper hair was parted in the middle, and she had a broad face, square jaw and no-nonsense demeanor.

I muttered, "Try to stay focused."

Fran shrugged and grinned sheepishly.

"We've divided you into groups of eight, and you'll be under the direction of team leaders. Each leader is equipped with a map, GPS unit and cell phone. As you search a grid, the eight of you will fan out, and you need to make sure there's adequate overlap between searchers. For those of you who are still filing in, we need you to check in at the registration table first. Everyone needs to have filled out a liability form, had a copy of their driver's license taken and been assigned to a team before we can allow you to join the search. Without the proper paperwork, we can't have you assisting us. Department rules."

Hillary turned to her left, toward a table underneath a blue tent. "That's our registration area. It'll be open until dark, so we can accommodate people who arrive throughout the day. Each foot search shift will last two hours or less, with a thirty-minute break in between. Don't push it. See how you feel at the end of your shift before you sign on for another. This is a marathon, not a sprint. Don't get carried away with adrenaline."

"Here." Fran tossed me a lavender bandana after I wiped sweat from my face with the back of my hand.

"One final note. I received word last night that our department has suspended all ground search operations until further notice. That means you're it. You're our eyes and feet, an invaluable asset to this investigation. We couldn't do it without you, and we appreciate you coming."

"You've given up!" a woman with a nose ring and a Mohawk shouted.

Her outburst was followed by someone yelling, "Kayla doesn't count!"

Hillary had started to hand the microphone to Destiny, but she pulled back, and her features hardened. "Kayla Martin counts. In the first hour after notification of her disappearance, we made reverse nine-one-one calls and had sixty officers assisting in door-to-door and yard searches. We covered this neighborhood with helicopters, planes with infrared technology and bloodhounds. On Friday, officers returned and retraced their steps, combing a one-mile radius from the point of origin. We haven't given up. We've merely narrowed the scope of our investigation in accordance with the evidence we've been presented. Other crimes have continued to occur in Highlands Ranch in the past three days, and we need to balance moving forward in this investigation with our current caseload."

Fran, who had hustled through the throngs, reached up and grabbed the microphone. "Fran Green here. Easy there, ladies. Get your heads in the game. We're here for one reason and one reason only. Kayla Martin. Keep that in mind."

With the exception of scattered rumblings, the crowd calmed.

"Couple more points to make," Fran added in a kinder tone. "Keep it clean today. Be respectful of the neighbors and neighborhood, and take care of yourselves with the sunscreen and water. Temperature might reach triple digits out on the asphalt. Don't want anyone wilting. Wear those orange safety vests. Might not look sexy, but could save your life. That's all I got. Be safe out there!"

I turned to head toward the search status board, where I'd been assigned for the day, but I pulled up when I felt a hand on my shoulder.

Destiny leaned in close, and I could smell her mango body wash.

"After everyone's been sent out, come find me," she whispered.

I looked at her searchingly. "Is everything okay?"

She shook her head. "I need to hire you and Fran."

"Now?"

"As soon as possible."

"For what?"

"To keep Gwen and Tracey from being arrested."

CHAPTER 2

Destiny Greaves wanted to hire me.

Given that Destiny and I had been romantically involved for four years, had lived under the same roof for three and had shared money and assets for two, technically that meant I would be hiring myself.

What if something went wrong? Would I have to fire myself? And Fran?

I couldn't begin to consider the possibilities. At the moment, I had duties to perform.

I aimed for the row of recreational vehicles, all of which belonged to members of the Rainbow Rangers traveling club, and returned to my position below the awning of a silver RV.

For the next hour, working in tandem with Jerri Alder, an outdoors enthusiast from Boulder, I updated the status board, a four-by-six dry-erase board we'd secured to a sturdy easel. As each team leader checked in, I recorded the zone number, description of the area to be searched, number of volunteers on the team and time of departure. The team leader then moved to a table a few feet away, where Jerri made marks on the map she and Fran had crafted overnight.

We dispatched twenty-two teams, after which Jerri delivered a monologue on the toxic effects of dog droppings on Boulder open space, and I pretended to care. Even though I was fascinated by the fact that she'd used a handheld GPS unit to record 3,150 piles of poop on a 300-yard section of a popular trail, I didn't have sufficient interest to spend ninety minutes on the subject. Luckily, team leaders broke the monotony by calling in or returning to the command center, where Jerri and I noted dozens of "significant finds."

Fruit snack wrappers and juice boxes were among the distinctive items volunteer searchers brought back, but apparently, the brands weren't ones typically purchased by Gwen Martin or Tracey Reid. A deflated balloon with a ribbon attached, a tennis ball, a Colorado Rockies cup and a section of an umbrella were also processed as evidence, but none of the items was recognized by either mother.

A crew of six women on ATVs took turns transporting bags of trash to a roped-off area north of the pavilion that had begun to resemble a landfill, but otherwise the morning passed slowly and uneventfully.

The highlight came when Destiny dropped by midway through my shift to tell me that Lieutenant Hillary Longhorn had passed on news that the Highlands Ranch police were treating Gwen Martin and Tracey Reid as "persons of interest."

The detective in charge of the investigation into Kayla Martin's disappearance, Destiny conveyed in a whisper, suspected someone at 8956 South Pine Lane of child abuse resulting in death.

Tracey Reid?

Gwen Martin?

Or both?

I never had a chance to ask Destiny, because she couldn't linger longer than sixty seconds.

Aware of the tension in her body, I reassured her again that I'd help however I could and reminded her that Fran would do the same. Destiny gave me a kiss on the cheek and hurried off in the direction of three satellite news trucks stationed on the perimeter of the park.

Child abuse resulting in death?

Not the best news when, in good faith, I'd sent off hundreds of women to search for Kayla. I'd lost count of the number who had voiced variations of, "I'll be out here until we find her," or, "I'll stay until they tell me to go."

At lunchtime, Fran completed her second shift of searching on foot and volunteered to relieve me at the board. I took her up on the offer and left in search of an office supply store, where I planned to purchase more dry-erase markers.

A big mistake, venturing onto suburban streets on my own.

Destiny had driven us to Founders Park in the dark that morning, when I'd barely been awake, much less paying attention. I'd always had a terrible sense of direction, which, fortunately didn't hinder me much in central Denver, where I lived and worked. In the heart of the city, parallel streets lined up nicely with the Rocky Mountains to the west. As a navigational bonus, some streets were clustered by presidents' names, famous universities, or American states, while others followed simple numerical or alphabetical order. Not too imaginative on the part of early settlers, but easy to follow.

Enter the suburbs, however, and all bets were off.

Highlands Ranch, a master-planned community in the southern corridor of the Denver metro area, stood as one of the worst examples of urban sprawl on the Front Range. Hundred-acre ranches had given way to thousands of houses, which spilled onto broad boulevards lined with big box stores. The area was known for its curved streets, odd-shaped lots, houses at every angle and rooftops that seemed to go on forever.

On the map, which I'd studied all morning, the neighborhoods in Highlands Ranch, with all their twists and turns, appeared to have been laid out by drunks. The street names, presumably designed to evoke images of wildlife and pristine open prairies, had the opposite effect. Thistle Ridge, Timberline Place, Quail Lane and Coyote Trail only served as reminders of what paving and progress had destroyed.

In my morning stint, I'd learned that more than 600 cul-de-sacs were part of the community, a statistic no one should have bragged about. A favorite of developers and homeowners because they reduced traffic and provided a safe environment for children to play, the dead-end streets also acted as barriers to neighbors getting to know each other. Ironically, they also forced too much togetherness. After four false starts trying to exit the Meadowridge subdivision, I fully understood the drawbacks to this type of development.

I also began to wonder how a stranger could have snatched Kayla Martin from her home or yard in broad daylight and escaped without notice.

That particular scenario seemed highly unlikely.

Forty-five minutes later, having completed my errands and returned to Founders Park, I poured potato chips onto my sandwich wrapper. "Why would anyone spend that much on a Winnebago?"

Fran took a bite of her sub, spilling toppings over the side. "Get with the program, Kris. It's a Grand Eaglebahn, forty-five foot, Class A coach."

"Six hundred thousand dollars?"

"Worth every penny. Nice funky shui."

"Funky shui?"

"Flow. Living room in front, kitchen and dining in the middle, bedroom and bath in the back. Get a load of the features. Five-hundred horse power, two-hundred-gallon tank, independent suspension."

"Whatever."

"Three air-conditioning units," Fran added, with her mouth full.

My eyes widened as I stared at the recreational vehicle where Gwen and Tracey had spent the morning. "Air-conditioning would be nice."

"Leather seats. Crown molding. Gold bath fixtures. Wool carpet. Flat-screen TVs. Oak cabinets. Stainless appliances." Fran sighed. "Was that luxury, or was I dreaming?"

I leaned closer. "You went inside?"

"Twice."

"Did you see Gwen and Tracey?" I whispered.

"Yep."

"How did they seem?"

"Aloof. Gave both of 'em hugs. Neither one hugged back."

"That's not surprising, is it, with what they're going through?"

Fran shook her head thoughtfully. "Something's off."

"Who's in there?"

"Just them. Destiny popped in and out a few times, but that's it."

"No one else? No friends or family?"

"Nope."

"Weird."

"Ain't it?"

"Destiny wants us to work for them."

Fran paused mid-chomp, exposing a mouthful of lettuce. "Doing what?"

"Clearing their names."

"Cops coming after 'em?"

I nodded. "How'd you know?"

"Makes sense. Last two to see Kayla alive. Bound to fall under the microscope of suspicion."

"Should we do it?" I asked, already having committed us. "Should we help them, for free?"

Fran cleaned her teeth with her tongue. "Might be tricky."

"Why?"

"Took a case while you were gone."

"Last week?"

"Friday morning."

"Why didn't you tell me?"

"Couldn't spill the beans over the phone. Didn't want to interfere with your grieving process."

"I hadn't seen my uncle in twenty-five years," I said curtly, referring to the man whose funeral I'd just attended in Seattle.

"Know how you hate to travel. Didn't want to work your nerves into a bundle before the return flight."

Now she had me nervous. "Is this a paying client?"

Fran took a gulp of Coke. "Full fee. Hourly plus expenses."

"What's involved?"

"Talk about it tomorrow. Back at the office."

"Fran!" I said, a warning in my tone.

She belched, without covering her mouth. "Hard to explain verbally. Need visuals."

"What visuals?"

Before Fran could reply, Arlene Tallon, a reporter from one of the local news stations, interrupted with an "itsy-bitsy" request.

Needless to say, I finished eating alone.

Fran accommodated Arlene Tallon by giving her a tour of the "guts of central command," bopping from the status board to the mapping area, from the evidence pile to the communications hub.

The two of them spent quite a bit of time in the RV that served as the focal point for communications—where laptops, color printers and copiers were being used to stay in touch with other activists and search organizations across the country—but they never entered the motor home that sheltered Gwen and Tracey.

Much to Fran's dismay, I'd turned down Arlene's offer to be interviewed on camera.

No good would have come from making my television debut on a day when my short brown hair was matted with sweat, my glasses were fogged with moisture from my eyebrows and my blue eyes were red from sleep deprivation. Not to mention, I didn't need the extra pounds the camera might have added to my five-six frame, not if the camera wouldn't add height. Just my luck, the taping would have added ten years, too, and I'd look as if I were pushing fifty, not forty, every wrinkle memorialized in high-definition.

Instead of preening like Fran, I concentrated on my search-status duties, and about an hour later, a woman with stringy red hair joined me as I made a mark on the dry-erase board.

"I need to take a load off."

"Feel free," I said, after she dropped into the collapsible camping chair Fran had vacated.

She let out an extended groan. "I'd be out searching, except I have a bad knee. My partner's on Team Seventeen. We always get involved with anything that has to do with the community. Any and every cause." She looked up at the board. "What're you doing?"

"Recording a potential piece of evidence that was found by Team Eleven."

"What is it?"

"An orange stuffed animal. Garfield, I believe."

"Where did they find it?"

"Under a bush on the median of Highlands Parkway."

She took a sip from a water bottle. "Did it belong to the girl?"

"Probably not."

"Then why are you recording it?"

"Because that's my job."

She cocked her head and studied me, head to toe. "Why don't you feel the stuffed animal's relevant?"

"Because none of the other twenty-six items I've recorded have been."

"Then why make notes? It's confusing."

"I'm following instructions."

"From whom?"

"Lieutenant Longhorn, the liaison from the Highlands Ranch Police Department."

The redhead pressed the water bottle against her forehead and wiped the moisture from it across her face. "Where is she?"

"She's on her way to show the animal to Kayla's mothers."

"Where are they?"

"In the black RV, the one with the yellow racing stripes."

"What're they doing in there?"

"I have no idea."

"If it were me, I'd be out searching for my daughter. I'd look until my feet blistered, and then I'd crawl on my hands and knees."

"Different people cope in different ways," I said mildly.

"What're the mothers like?"

"I haven't met them."

"Huh." She rubbed her left knee. "I wonder if they had anything to do with it."

"Kayla's disappearance? Why would you think that?"

"I get hunches. My friends say I have intuitive abilities, and I should develop them."

"Okay," I said, distracted.

I was busy watching Lieutenant Longhorn, tracking her every step as she moved from the police truck positioned near the pavilion to the steps of the black RV, the Garfield toy in her hand.

Seconds later, a high-pitched scream drowned out the pattering of my companion.

CHAPTER 3

"May as well get it over with," Fran said the next morning, tossing a large envelope onto my desk.

I looked at the Betty Boop clock behind her head. The little hand was on the seven, and the big hand had yet to reach the twelve. I hadn't even been in the office two minutes, and I was having trouble adjusting to the bright light streaming in through the windows and to the explosion of colors on Fran's desk.

Our office, situated on Sixth Avenue, was the middle unit in a one-story brick row house, tucked between a flower shop and a secondhand clothing store.

Whereas I preferred to come into a clean, stark environment every morning, with hardwood floors, exposed brick and track lighting serving as sufficient decoration, Fran was a nester. The top of her desk had a Zen raking garden, a gumball machine, a Galileo thermometer and assorted specimens from her latest craze: geodes. Recently, Fran had tried to bleed into my desk space with a handful of sports and entertainment figures from her bobblehead collection, but when I transferred them—upside down—into the freezer door, she'd abandoned that practice.

"I assume whatever's in that envelope relates to the case you accepted on Friday?"

"Does indeed. Friend of mine, Margaret Bogan, hired me. Her daughter Chelsey went to cheerleading camp, weekend before last in Vail."

"Good for her." After fifteen hours at the status board the day before, another one lost in transit and two spent packing and unpacking at the park and home, my feet were killing me, my head ached and my stomach burned.

When I refused to open the envelope, Fran reached over to retrieve it, pulled out a photograph and held it six inches from my face. "Teeny bopper brought back some pictures from the trip."

My eyes bulged. "What the hell is that?"

"What's it look like?"

"This isn't funny. Where'd you get it?" I snatched the picture and rotated it several times, in an effort to determine which side was up.

"From the kid's camera. Told you, Chelsey attended a cheerleading camp."

"A teenager took this picture?"

"Says she didn't."

"Who did?"

"Chelsey claims she doesn't know. Mother's beside herself. That's why she's hired me, to get to the bottom of it."

I threw the photo to the side of my desk. "This is another one of your Photoshop tricks, isn't it?"

Fran made the sign of the cross in front of her chest. "Not this time. Telling you, Chelsey found this when she loaded the pics onto her computer."

I couldn't stop glancing at the image. "You swear this isn't a joke?"

"Wouldn't pull a prank on you. Well, might," she corrected herself. "But not today. Like it or not, this is for real. Best I can make out, someone swiped Chelsey's camera from her room at the Mountain Chalet in Vail and had some fun with it."

"What's that purple thing?"

"Chelsey's purse."

I winced. "Someone posed with a purse?"

"Must have. Plenty of other artistic touches, too, what with the water bottle and iPod. Kid wants to throw away everything that was touched."

"I would, too," I said as the phone on Fran's desk rang.

She looked at Caller ID, motioned for me to be quiet and picked up the receiver.

I shook my head, unable to believe that I was staring at a full-color close-up of a vagina.

Fran said loudly, "Green here. Hold on a sec, John." She covered the phone and whispered to me. "Gotta take this call."

"Right this minute?"

"Sit tight. Been playing phone tag with this fellow since yesterday morning. Take but a second."

"Fine."

I rose to head toward the water dispenser, but she grabbed me by the arm. "Don't go anywhere. Want you in on this."

I plopped back into my chair. "What now?"

Fran raised the volume on the side of the phone. "Putting you on speaker, John. My partner's here in the office with me. Kristin Ashe, meet John Whately, director of the Loralei Recovery Foundation, world headquarters in Dallas."

I shot Fran a questioning look but said politely, "Nice to meet you."

"You, too, ma'am."

"Kris is the lead private eye on the Martin case. Was out of town last week attending a family funeral, but cut short her trip. I've brought her up to speed. The good news make it down to the Lone Star state? You get my e-mail?"

"Yes, and it's encouraging to hear that you found a stuffed animal that might have belonged to the missing child. It sounds promising."

"Waiting for confirmation, but all in all, had a productive day. Hit forty-two of our fifty-five targeted areas. Would've done more, but the heat got to some of the gals. Managed to polish off five subdivisions, about nine square miles total. Can't wait to get you and your crew up here next weekend. With the warm bodies you're bringing, we'll super-size those parameters."

"About that," John began. "There's been a change in plans. I'm afraid we'll have to scale back our participation."

"You won't be sending two busloads of folks to Colorado to help search for Kayla?"

"Er, no. That won't be possible."

Fran frowned. "One?"

"I'm afraid I mistook the level of interest."

"Cut to the chase. How many volunteers are coming?"

"None."

"No one's coming?" Fran practically yelled.

"I'm afraid not."

She clenched her teeth and shook her head. "What brought this on?"

"I'm sorry. Truly I am, but our organization can't afford a public association with the type of search you're conducting."

"What type would that be?"

John cleared his throat. "One that involves an unusual domestic situation."

"Two lesbians as mothers, that's got your tighty-whities in a ball?"

"The lifestyle choices are challenging . . ." he replied, his voice trailing off.

"You're telling me that missing children of lesbian parents don't deserve to be found? You want to say that on record?"

"Of course they do, but—"

"Made it clear to you from the beginning that Kayla Martin had two mothers. Gwen Martin and Tracey Reid. Women, both of them. Full disclosure."

"Yes, but I misjudged the degree of concern from our supporters. We run a faith-based organization. Most of our volunteers have good Christian values—"

"Let me stop you right there," Fran said tersely. "Spent thirty years in a convent, so don't open that can of worms with me. Tell me this: Ain't it the stated mission of your foundation to help other communities organize and staff searches for missing children?"

"Yes, but—"

"Didn't read any qualifiers or disclaimers on the paperwork you sent me."

"No, but—"

"Ain't you supposed to be ready to kick into gear within days of a child being reported missing?"

"Yes, but—"

"Ain't your long-term, stated goal, and I quote, 'To scare every perpetrator in every community into thinking a broad search can be mobilized on a moment's notice?' I get that right?"

"Yes, but—"

"'Never give up until the missing are found.' Ain't that your motto?"

"Yes, but—"

"Didn't I read all this hogwash on your Web site? Didn't I hear it coming out of your mouth two days ago?"

"Yes, but—"

"Or was I talking to an imposter?"

"If you'd let me finish," John said, sounding aggrieved. "I did make those comments, but since that time, I've been pressured by our board."

"Pressured how?"

"They're concerned that any involvement in Colorado could affect future donations to our foundation. If our funding were to shrink, that, in turn, would jeopardize our ability to conduct searches in other communities."

"Those matter more? Some kid who's safe at home, this very minute, is more important to you than a little girl we know is missing? Out there alone and terrified or dead and disposed of?"

"I'm not saying that," he replied helplessly. "You're putting words in my mouth."

"Try these on for size. I assume this Loralei, the namesake for your foundation, she had a mom and a dad?"

"Yes."

Fran stabbed at the phone with her two middle fingers. "Guess she was born into the right kind of family. Bully for her."

"That's not fair," John protested.

Fran exploded. "You lecturing me on fair?" I motioned for her to calm down, but she continued in a violent voice. "This anti-gay stance might harm your fundraising. You ever consider that?"

"It's out of my control. All I can do is express my deepest sympathies to the family and wish you the best. Truly, I am sorry."

"You will be if Kayla Martin's body turns up——"

"I have to go."

"——and you could have done something to prevent it."

"I'll pray for you."

"You do that!" Fran shouted, before picking up the receiver and slamming it back into its cradle.

Fran paced for a full five minutes, becoming redder by the second.

In the beginning, she ranted at the top of her lungs, often evoking the word God, and never in a positive context. Then she stomped back and forth muttering under her breath, scrubbing her gray crew cut as if she needed to rid it of lice.

I knew her well enough not to interrupt, and eventually, she ran out of steam and collapsed into her high-back, leather chair. "Sorry about breaking the phone."

"Don't worry. We have a spare in the supply closet."

"Damn that son of a bitch! Trying to out-Christian me! The nerve!"

"We'll find Kayla," I said in a placating tone. "With or without John Whately and his group."

"You think so?"

"Of course," I lied.

"Dead or alive?"

"I don't know."

"Screw that poser and his merry band of marauders. Where were we?"

"Obscene photographs, taken with a cheerleader's camera."

"Sure enough." Fran reached into the envelope again.

This time, she handed me five photographs, and I rifled through them. Whoever had snapped the shots had been careful to take pictures that displayed legs and genitals only, with Chelsey Bogan's personal items artfully staged. For the record, a vagina, surrounded by a teenager's everyday items, was not as stimulating as it might have sounded.

Morbidly fascinating? Yes.

Arousing? No.

I sighed. "Do we have to take this case?"

"Said I would." Fran shrugged. "Chelsey could be at risk, but you want I should turn it down?"

"Maybe. How long will it take?"

"Shouldn't be a big deal. Figure I'll have a chat with Chelsey and the two other girls who shared the room at the Chalet. Take a look at the pictures on the disk. Nail down a time line for when these babies were snapped. See who had access to the hotel room. Can't tell from the background if the shots were taken in the room or somewhere else. Have to track down the movements of the camera," she said, as she pushed aside a glazed donut and made a note on her desk blotter. "What you got planned for today?"

"At nine o'clock, I'm meeting with Gwen and Tracey."

"You need me there?"

"No. Preliminary interviews are usually more effective one-on-one."

"Why?" Fran said, scratching her head.

"Why don't I need you?"

"Why Chelsey Bogan? Don't all our investigations open with that devil of a word and close with money, love or revenge?"

"Most," I agreed.

"Aye or nay? Keep moving forward or back out?"

I'd had enough of pubic hair and veins. I put the photos back in the envelope and handed them to Fran. "Find out who the hell this is."

In less than ninety minutes, I was standing on the covered front porch of the two-story house at 8956 South Pine Lane, surveying the other seven houses on the cul-de-sac.

Most of the subdivisions in Highlands Ranch, including Meadowridge, had been constructed in the 1980s, a period when developers had introduced great rooms, kitchen islands, built-in entertainment centers, master bedroom retreats and association-maintained front yards.

I would have loved to have had any and all of those amenities included in the three-story, brick mansion I shared with Destiny and two sets of tenants in Denver's historic Capitol Hill neighborhood, but I'd always felt the tradeoff was too high.

Were the buyers who moved into these pressed-paper suburban houses blind?

Or more to the point, did they bother to look out their blinds? While builders had added ample cosmetic perks, they'd also made three-car garages and concrete driveways focal points. Worse, they'd built houses too big on lots too small, with a communistic sameness distinguished only by pre-ordained color patterns.

I wondered why Gwen Martin and Tracey Reid had chosen to raise their daughter in such a place, on a block where I would have felt out of place, no matter how many years I lasted.

I waved at a lady across the street who was retrieving a newspaper from her front yard, but she didn't return the courtesy. Instead, she scurried back into her California Contemporary, the pale yellow twin to the Martin-Reid's olive green version.

I rang the bell, and after a short delay, Tracey opened the door.

In her hands, she held an orange stuffed animal.

CHAPTER 4

"She's dead," Tracey eked out a few minutes later, her voice hoarse.

I'd been moving crayons and colored pencils to make room for my legal pad, but I paused and looked at her carefully. She was dressed in baggy sweats and a rugby shirt. Her curly hair was greasy, and her acne-scarred skin had an unhealthy tint to it. "You don't know that."

"I know it in my heart. If Kayla were alive, I'd feel something, and I don't."

"You're under tremendous stress—"

Her gaze was unflinching. "They won't find her alive. Too much time has passed."

"Don't give up."

"The police have. I heard two officers talking yesterday. They said if a child isn't found within forty-eight hours, odds are she'll be found dead, if she's found at all."

"Practically every lesbian in Denver is looking for Kayla. That'll help the odds."

She blew her nose, which was red and swollen. "Destiny wants to keep drawing attention to my daughter, but I just want the phone to ring, for it to be over. I need a body to complete my mourning."

"You should trust Destiny's instincts. She's rarely wrong."

Tracey fiddled with one of the three keyboards on her L-shaped desk. We were in a twelve-foot square room upstairs, in the southwest corner of the house, sitting on drafting chairs in front of cherry desks and hutches. I was at one proportioned for a child, while Tracey was positioned in front of an executive-sized work station. The equipment on the desktop—two hard drives, three monitors, a television and a power generator—seemed to dwarf her.

"How did Kayla's Garfield get on that median?" she asked.

"I don't know. When did you last see it?"

"I can't remember."

"The one you're holding is similar to it?"

Tracey nodded slightly. "Gwen went out and bought it this morning."

"You're certain the one searchers found yesterday belonged to Kayla?"

"Positive. It was missing one eye and both ears and the whiskers. Kayla used to pick at it when she was a baby. The top of the right leg matched, too. Last week, I stitched the thigh when the stuffing started to fall out." Tracey covered her mouth with a fist. "Gwen will never forgive me. No matter how this turns out."

"I'm sure that's not true."

"I can hear it in her voice," she said in a resigned tone. "I feel it when she hugs me. We're going through the motions."

"You shouldn't blame yourself."

"How can I not? Everyone else has."

"Is there anything I can do?"

She looked perplexed. "Do?"

"Anything that might comfort you?"

"Um, no," she said, her eyes fixed on two framed photos in the hutch. In one, Kayla was on top of Tracey's shoulders, holding an ice cream cone with sprinkles. In the other, she was running toward the camera, a large rubber ball poking out from beneath her shirt. "Gwen's her real mother," Tracey added abruptly.

"Pardon?"

"Gwen gave birth to Kayla. That's the first thing everyone wants to know. A friend of hers—former friend now—was the sperm donor."

"You've had a falling out with the biological father?"

Tracey nodded. "Over visitation rights."

"What happened?"

"We cut him off in February. He kept asking for more time with Kayla, but he would cancel the dates we gave him. Children need structure, and he was too permissive. Every time Kayla came home from a visit with him, she was mouthy and ill-behaved. Legally, according to the papers we signed before Kayla was born, Bruce doesn't have any rights. We decided to enforce our original agreement."

"What's Bruce's last name?"

"McCarthy."

"Where does he live?"

"In Capitol Hill, at Eighth and Grant."

I made a note. "Could Bruce have had something to do with Kayla's disappearance?"

She shrugged. "I'm the wrong person to ask. I never wanted to use his sperm, but Gwen insisted. She wanted the father to be someone we'd met, someone our child could meet."

"I know you've probably been over this repeatedly, but could you tell me what happened on Thursday?"

"What do you need to know?"

"Anything you can remember. From the beginning of the day."

Tracey blinked rapidly and took a few quick breaths. "Gwen got up at seven and woke up Kayla."

"Was that their typical time?"

"That's their routine when Gwen's in town."

"She travels a lot?"

"Every other week," Tracey said, clearing her throat. "She's a soft-ware engineer for Verizon, and they send her all over the country. When she's home, she lets Kayla play in the bathroom while she's getting ready, then she wakes me up before she leaves for work."

"Which she did?"

"Mmm, hmm."

"What next?"

"Kayla and I ate breakfast, and we spent the morning inside."

"Doing what?"

"Kayla watched *Dora* and *Scooby Doo*, and I worked in here. I don't normally let her watch that much television, but I'd been trying to catch up on my work. I do freelance closed-captioning."

"Go on."

"Around noon, we ate lunch, outside on the back patio. Then we put together her *Beauty and the Beast* puzzle, and I read a book to her, then tucked her in bed. In the top bunk. She's just started sleeping there, for naps."

"Can she get in and out of the bed by herself?"

Tracey nodded. "She uses the ladder."

"What book did you read?"

"*What Next?* It's a picture book about a high-spirited kitten. Kayla loves to guess what the kitty's going to do next. Before I turn the page, she knows when he's carrying underwear around the house or turning on the water in the bathtub." Tracey paused to cough, emitting a painful sound. She hurriedly grabbed a handful of tissues from the box on her desk and spit into the wad. "Sorry. I've been sick for almost two weeks. I caught it from Kayla. She had greenish-brown crud coming out of her nose for days, and then I came down with it. I've been coughing up pea-size chunks of this crap. I felt like hell Thursday. After I put Kayla to bed, I tried to work some more, but I couldn't concentrate. I felt nauseous and started to get the chills, so I put on three sweaters and went back to the computer. When my teeth kept chattering, I gave up, took NyQuil and went to bed."

"How much NyQuil?"

"I can't really remember, but I felt rotten. Normally, I'm a light sleeper. If I hadn't been medicated, I would have heard something. I'm sure I would have," she said in a monotone. "I should have called Gwen and made her come home from work."

"What time did you wake up?"

"At four sixteen. I remember looking at the clock and being surprised it was that late. I went to look in on Kayla, and when I saw she wasn't in her room, I knew she was gone."

"Right away?"

"Yes."

"Did the room look disturbed?"

"No, but I had this awful feeling."

"Did you call nine-one-one?"

"Not that second. I ran through the house, out to the backyard, through the gate and over to the neighbors' house. I was just running. That's all I remember. Running."

"Which neighbors?"

Tracey pointed toward the south. "The Fraziers."

"They're friends of yours?"

"We're not close, but their daughter Sierra likes to play with Kayla."

"They're the same age?"

"No. Sierra's in third grade. She'd come home from school. I saw her through her bedroom window, but she wouldn't answer the door. I screamed at her, asking if she'd seen Kayla, but she just shook her head. After that, I ran home and called nine-one-one."

"Was Sierra home alone?"

"I don't know. Usually she is, at that time of day. Kim, her mom, works until six, and her dad hasn't lived with them in months."

"How much time elapsed between when you woke up and when you placed the nine-one-one call?"

"No more than five minutes."

"Destiny told me that the police are focusing on a supposed delay in reporting."

Tracey let out a weary sigh. "The dispatcher confused me. She asked when Kayla went missing, and I said at one o'clock, meaning that's when I'd last seen her. When I put her down for her nap. They're twisting my words. I was out of my mind with fear. I don't know what I said."

"Did you notice anything unusual on the street that day?"

"The police have already asked me these questions."

"Please, one more time."

"The people across the street were having their carpets cleaned. A van was parked in the driveway."

"What are their names?"

"I don't know. We haven't met yet. They moved in last month, into the yellow house that's the same model as ours."

"Did you notice the name of the cleaning business?"

"No, but the van was white with red lettering, if that helps."

"It might." I jotted down the details. "Did anything else happen on Thursday, anything out of the ordinary?"

"Not that I noticed."

"How about in the past weeks or month? Has anything struck you as unusual?"

"Only the strange man I told the police about, but I haven't seen him recently."

"What strange man?"

"Some man in his sixties started showing up at Founders Park a while back. He came every day and sat near the playground equipment, pretending to read a newspaper."

I felt a chill. "How do you know he was pretending?"

Tracey sniffled. "Kayla noticed it one day, after he made a point of greeting her. She whispered to me that he never opened the paper."

"When did you last see him? Can you try to remember?"

"It's been at least two weeks. Kayla and I have been too sick to go anywhere."

"The police are checking up on that lead?"

"They said they would."

"Thursday afternoon, were the doors locked?"

"The front, not the back. We only lock the sliding glass door at night."

"Do you have a lock on the gate?" I asked, referring to the gate I'd seen on the southern portion of the six-foot wooden fence that enclosed the back and side yards.

"Not a lock, but there's a latch, high up, and it's always fastened."

"Kayla couldn't have reached it?"

"No. Do you think the police are looking into my background?"

"Probably, but that's common in these types of investigations. You shouldn't worry about it."

"It might be a problem." Tracey swallowed hard. "I used to hang with a rough crowd."

I kept my voice calm. "When?"

"Before I met Gwen, and it won't help to ask me any questions. I don't remember half of what I did or who I did it with." Tracey stared out the window for a long time before adding, "I was a meth addict."

CHAPTER 5

"One of Kayla's mothers was addicted to methamphetamine," I said to Fran shortly after Tracey dropped the bombshell on me. Even though I was locked inside my car, with the windows rolled up, two hundred feet from the house, I whispered the words into my cell phone.

I heard Fran's sharp intake of breath. "Son of a gun. Which one?"

"Tracey."

"She 'fess up, or someone else rat her out?"

"She told me."

"Clean now?"

"I hope so. She went through rehab five years ago."

"Smokin' or cookin'?"

"Both."

"Cripes! That's a buzz kill."

"We weren't exactly floating on cloud nine before the revelation."

"Speak for yourself. Got some great news after you left. What would you think about greasing this investigation with fifty K?"

"In fees?"

"Don't you wish! Try a reward and tip line. Heavy hitter in the lesbo community's offered to kick in the cash. Destiny's setting up a phone line, arranging publicity, pressing to hit the noon news."

"You think money will help?"

"You kidding? Watch those lips loosen. You know what I love about the big green? Makes bad people do good things. Sit tight, and Kayla'll be back in her bed before lights out."

I put the key in the ignition, and when I cracked the driver's window, I was struck by how quiet it seemed outside. I heard none of the usual sounds I was accustomed to at my house—horns honking, sirens wailing, car doors slamming, grocery carts wheeling, Dumpster lids clanking. It was as if the Highlands Ranch neighborhood were deserted.

"Who put up the money for the reward?"

"Gal by the name of Wren Priestly. Fifty-something, retired mogul. Made her fortune in the dot-com boom, pulled out before the bust. Worth upward of a hundred million according to articles in the *Denver Post*. Wouldn't mind a taste of that myself."

"The woman or her fortune?"

Fran chuckled. "Both."

"You contacted her?"

"Nope. She called the Lesbian Community Center on her own. Me, never have made her acquaintance in person. Has an entourage around her every time she appears in public, which ain't often. Likes her bling. Heavy gold ropes and bangles."

"What's the catch?"

"No catch. Just wants the name of her nonprofit, The United Lesbian Foundation, attached to the effort. Makes that a criterion whenever she gives, and this bird gives a lot. Sprinkles her money all across America. Be glad some of it came our way."

"I am. I'm just concerned that we might get overwhelmed with false tips."

"Count on that. Let's start with what we know. Fill me in."

After I summarized what I'd learned that morning, Fran made a sucking noise. "Let me get this straight in my head. Two possibilities. Someone entered the premises, or Kayla exited on her own."

"Correct."

"Let's go with the first theory. Point of entry had to be the back door. Front was locked. Okay, kidnapper's inside. What next?"

"He or she takes Kayla."

"No signs or sounds of a struggle."

"Kayla could have been asleep, or—"

"Could have left with someone she knew," Fran said, sounding pumped. "Good. Next theory, Kayla left on her own. Through the front door or—"

"She couldn't have. The door was locked when Tracey woke up."

"Nix that. Through the back door, but then what? Thought you said the gate was latched."

"It was, but on my way out, I tested it. If you jostle it, it opens. The latch comes undone by itself."

"Easily?"

"Fairly."

"Let's run with that. Kayla voluntarily leaves the backyard, loses her way and is lying out there somewhere, injured or scared. Maybe under a bush or in thick grass."

"I doubt it. The police searched on Thursday and Friday. We searched yesterday."

"It could happen. Sprite of a thing got lost. Felt tired, laid down."

"If a three-year-old had started crying, forty people would have come out of their houses. This isn't the middle of the National Forest."

Fran let out a sigh. "Make a point there. Brings us to the more dire scenario."

"Someone picked her up."

"Crime of opportunity, and that train of thought splits down two tracks. Bad and worse. Distraught woman takes Kayla in order to create or replace a child. Or a pervy man—"

"Don't go there."

"Fact of life."

My head started pounding. "I know."

"Perp angle doesn't feel right," Fran said thoughtfully. "Sicko couldn't have watched the family, scoped out the lay of the land. Not from that dead-end street with no alley. No way, no how. Whoever took Kayla must have been known to her. Let's go with that angle. Can't do much about a stranger anyway. Not our realm of expertise. Let's zero in on what we can control."

"People known to Kayla."

"Yep. Friends, family, acquaintances. We'll interview 'em quick as we can, starting with the bio father. Might have decided to award himself custody. Give me his name again."

"Bruce McCarthy."

"Current or last known address?"

"Eighth and Grant."

"Denver? Our neck of the woods?"

"Yes. Can you run a background check on him?"

"Done. Pre-authorization for rush service charges?"

"Of course."

"Just checking."

"Fran!"

"Always got your eye on the bottom line. Running a business, not a charity. That's what you say at every shareholders meeting."

"We are now."

"Righto, boss! Got me another idea for Brucie."

"What?"

"New investigative technique I learned last month. New to you and me, should have said. Oldie but goodie in the private-eye industry."

"What is it?"

"Hate to spoil the surprise. Dirty work, that's all I'm saying. We'll go out under the cover of darkness. Don't you worry your pretty little head. Just be in my truck by ten."

"Fine."

"While I'm at it, any other names you want fed through the databases?"

"One more. Shelby Valentine."

"Spelled like it sounds?"

"Yes."

"Current or last known address?"

"Tracey didn't have one."

"Relationship?"

"Ex-lover."

"Nasty split?"

"Tracey wouldn't give me any details."

"No worries. Twenty-four hours or less, and I'll have the skinny. Gwen toss in any names?"

"I haven't seen her this morning."

"Don't tell me she went to work."

"She's taken a leave of absence. Right now, she's out looking for Kayla."

"Where?"

"Just wandering. According to Tracey, she's done this every day since Kayla went missing."

"Not healthy. When's she due back?"

"Tracey doesn't know."

"Ring her on her cell."

"I can't. Gwen doesn't take it with her."

"Can't be true! What mum would leave behind her communication lifeline at a time like this? Makes no sense."

"I'm just telling you what Tracey told me."

"Dang. They're cracking up down there in suburbia. I better come by and get that house in order. Got to stop by Chelsey's school first, though. Meeting with the three girls who shared the room in Vail. Then the day's wide open. Bring my laptop, work out of the house and keep an eye on the gals. While I'm there, might have a chance to check out the carpet cleaner situation and the weirdo in the park."

"Gwen and Tracey might not want company."

"Nonsense. Grieving people need someone to watch over them. Friends and family ain't flocking around, right?"

"No. They're not," I said, my attention pulled in a different direction. A white passenger van had parked behind my Honda Accord, and I watched as men, women and children emptied out of it.

"Any spare rooms in the house?"

"One in the basement, but—"

"Tell the mothers I'm coming."

I squinted to read the sign a woman in a long skirt held in front of her breasts. "You might want to get here as soon as you can."

Fran said lightheartedly, "You missing me that much?"

My heart started racing. "A group of protestors just arrived."

In no time, the clan from Sacred Life Church began to silently march back and forth on the sidewalk in front of Kayla Martin's house.

I stepped out of my car and exchanged a few choice words with them, but then held my tongue when I saw a young girl sitting on a glider on the front porch of the Fraziers' house. She had wavy golden hair and big teeth with a slight overbite. On her skinny frame, she wore a purple tube top and pink shorts that barely covered her underpants. Her arms and legs were bright white, with strips of sunburn covering the fronts.

I walked toward the porch, and the girl called out, "You shouldn't say bad words."

The rottweiler that was spread out on the steps, lifted its tan eyebrows at my approach. "Sorry about that." I bent to scratch the dog's ears. "What's his name?"

"*Her* name's Cookie."

"You must be Sierra."

The girl's eyes widened. "How did you know? I saw you at Kayla's house. Are you her friend?"

"I'm friends with her moms. I'm Kristin."

"Oh."

"How come you're not in school today?"

Sierra jerked her feet on the porch, causing the glider to swing furiously. "I'm sick."

I sat on the porch rail, my back to the street. "What's wrong?"

"I threw up."

"Mmm."

"I made myself do it," she added.

"Why? Don't you like school?"

"It's okay, but I like Tae Kwon Do better. I have my brown belt."

"Good for you."

She jumped up. "Want to see me kick something?"

"Maybe later."

"When?"

"Probably never," I admitted.

Her face fell. "You don't like martial arts?"

"Not especially. Why didn't you want to go to school today?"

"I wanted to stay home, so I could play with Kayla."

I looked at Sierra with concern. "You know she's missing, don't you?"

She shrugged. "They'll find her, and then we can play in my tree house. My dad made it, but he doesn't live here anymore."

"How come?"

"My mom said he shouts too much," she said, kicking at the porch railing. "He has his own apartment now."

"Where does he live?"

"By Target."

"Do you see him much?"

"Sometimes." Sierra snapped her fingers, and Cookie rose and stretched. "Want to see my tree house? It's in the backyard."

"Maybe we should ask your mom first. Is she home?"

"She's at work. She's a lawyer."

"Who's watching you?"

"Me."

"All day long?"

Sierra nodded, covering her eyes to shield them from the glare of the sun. "My mom says I talk too much. That's why I have my own house. Want to come?"

"Sure," I said, casting a backward glance at the protestors.

"I'm on a diet," she announced as she grabbed my hand and pulled me toward the side yard.

"How's that going?" I said, careful not to reveal anything in my tone.

"I've lost twelve pounds." Sierra tiptoed from flagstone to flagstone. "I exercise at least once a day, and I don't eat as much junk food. I weigh myself twice a day."

I stopped walking, which tugged her to an abrupt halt. "Does your mom know?"

She made a face. "Don't tell her. She gave me a scale for my birthday, but she took it away. I bought another one at a garage sale for three dollars and hid it in my closet. I'm not supposed to exercise on purpose. My mom says I'm too skinny, but she's just jealous because she's so fat. I have to lose six more pounds."

"Don't do that. You look fine."

"No! If I eat two M&Ms, my stomach gets bigger."

"I doubt that."

"Yes, it does!"

"If it gets any smaller," I observed, "it'll be concave."

"What's that?"

"Sunk in."

"That's what I want," Sierra said, patting her stomach and brightening. "Concave."

She led us through the gate that had been propped open with a brick and into the backyard, where there wasn't a tree in sight. There was, however, a gorgeous Cape Cod playhouse with four-pane windows, black shutters, taupe-colored siding and a red Dutch door.

I let out a long whistle. "This is much nicer than the fort I had when I was a kid."

"It's not a fort," Sierra said haughtily as we scooted through the door and settled on pillows on the carpeted floor. "I told you. It's a tree house."

She proceeded to offer me an apple juice box from the mini-fridge in the corner of the eight-foot-by-twelve-foot playhouse. I took a sip out of the straw I'd punched through the top of the box and eyed the television, radio/CD player, built-in day bed, lamp and curtains. "What do you do out here?"

"Draw. Read. Watch TV. Play Gameboy. Talk on my cell phone. Play with my dog," she said in a stream. "My mom says I'm not allowed to have more than one friend in the tree house at a time. And no boys."

"How would she know?"

Sierra pointed to a device suspended from the ceiling, in the corner of the room, and waved. "That's a webcam. My mom can see me from her office."

My eyes bulged, a move I hoped the camera didn't catch. "Is that a diary?" I said, referring to a pink book on the daybed.

She nodded. "I write in it every day."

"What do you write?"

"Stuff. I have a boyfriend. His name is Drake. He comes up to here," she said, touching her nose.

"Okay."

She motioned to her neck. "My other boyfriend, Cole, only came to here. We broke up, but he's going to marry my best friend Angela."

I could barely conceal a grimace. "Soon?"

"Next week. They have a wedding planner. My other best friend Shaunique. Want to see a picture of Drake?"

"Your old boyfriend?"

Sierra let out an exasperated sigh. "My new one."

"I guess."

She reached into her pink purse and pulled out a wrinkled photograph. "He's in the middle." She used a purple fingernail to indicate a boy with freckles and a cowlick.

"Who was that?" I said, indicating the space where someone had been cut from the group photo.

"Stacia. We don't like her anymore."

"Why?"

"No reason."

I handed back the photo. "Did you write in your diary last Thursday?"

"Yes," Sierra said, elongating the word. "I told you I write every day."

"What did you write?"

"About the police cars on the street. There were six. I counted them."

"Were they here when you got home from school?"

"Later."

"What time did you come home?"

"Two thirty. That's when I always come home from school."

"Every day? By yourself?"

Sierra nodded in slow motion. "My mom makes me comes straight home, and I have to call her before I can go in my tree house."

"Did you see Kayla that day?"

"No. She's a baby. She still sucks her thumb."

"Did you see anyone else hanging around on Thursday afternoon?"

"Like who?" she said, looking confused.

"Someone you'd never seen before? A man or a woman? Or maybe a boy or girl?"

"Nuh, unh."

"When was the last time you saw Kayla?"

She waved her hands. "A long, long time ago."

"I understand you like to play with her."

"I used to, but I'm not allowed to when she's sick."

"Is that what her moms told you?"

"Yeah."

"Do you like Kayla's moms?"

Sierra scratched her nose. "I guess. They're sort of nice. I like

Tracey best."

"Do you spend a lot of time at their house?"

"When they let me."

"You said your dad shouts a lot. Do you ever hear Gwen or Tracey shouting?"

"No."

"Have you ever seen one of them be mean to Kayla?"

"Maybe."

My pulse quickened. "When?"

"When Kayla's bad, they make her have a time-out. She has to go to her room and stay until she stops crying and says she's sorry."

"Does that take long?"

Sierra seemed to be staring at something over my left shoulder. "Not too long. I know why Kayla has two moms."

"Why?"

"Because her moms don't like men."

"How do you know that?"

"I heard my mom tell my aunt. That's why."

"Actually, Kayla has two moms because they love each other and they love Kayla."

"They're not a real family," Sierra interjected.

She seemed to be watching for my reaction, but I remained expressionless. "Did you hear that from your mom, too?"

"No. Someone else."

"Who?"

"Ben's mom and dad. They live over there." Sierra pointed in the direction of a house behind us. "I miss Kayla."

"What do you miss about her?"

"Her," Sierra said matter-of-factly. She fiddled with Cookie's paws, folding and unfolding them. "I know where Kayla's hiding."

Goose bumps formed on my arm. "Where?"

"I'm not supposed to tell."

"Why not?"

"If you count to ten and yell, 'Ready or not, here I come,' you can go find her."

"It's not that simple—" I began, stopping when I heard musical notes.

Sierra reached into her purse to answer her cell phone, silencing the ringtone.

After responding to the caller with several monosyllabic words, she whispered to me, "My mom says you have to leave."

CHAPTER 6

"How bad is it?" Destiny said to me five minutes later.

I was back in my car, and I'd driven off Pine Lane and parked on Spruce Drive, where the residences backed up to the Martin-Reid and Frazier properties.

"Fran called you?"

"Immediately. Why didn't you?"

"I'm a little busy here," I said with irritation. "I called the police, but they said there's nothing illegal going on, as long as the protestors don't trespass on private property. The dispatcher told me that she'd send an officer to assess the situation, but no one's shown up."

"When was that?"

"Twenty minutes ago."

"What's going on?"

"There are about thirty people. Some are standing in the middle of the street, holding signs and shouting. Others are participating in a moving Mass."

"A Mass? On the street?"

"On the sidewalk. You should see it. The cul-de-sac's shaped like a lightbulb, with Gwen and Tracey's house on the top. The minister starts at one end, and as he walks backward, a clump of people follow. He passes the eight houses on the street, then turns around. They all gather again and retrace their steps. They're reading from Mass books as they walk, calling out refrains."

"Jesus Christ! What do the signs say?"

"Shit like, 'God cannot be bought.'"

"What's that mean?"

"I have no idea. Another choice one is, 'There won't be any anti-discrimination laws to protect you in hell.'"

"Do they have loudspeakers?"

"No, and they don't need them. One gnarled old man stands on a wooden cube, and he has this obnoxious voice that practically carries to Colorado Springs. He yells, 'Homosexual child abusers live here.'"

"Oh, God," Destiny said wearily.

"There are three kids, ranging in age from four to ten, give or take, and they're screaming, 'Mommy, mommy, I want a daddy.'"

"Have there been any altercations?"

"Just one, verbal."

"Between?"

I paused for a moment. "Me and them."

"Stop, honey! A confrontation won't help."

"What am I supposed to do when I see a sign that says, 'Wherever she is, Kayla's in a better place'?"

"Tolerate it."

"But—"

"For the moment. I promise you we'll respond, starting with a candlelight vigil. I'm already getting the word out. Tonight at eight."

"Here?"

"On Gwen and Tracey's front lawn, spilling into the street. I want the public to see our show of solidarity."

"Are you sure that's a good idea? Tracey seems to—"

"Let me do my job, Kris, and you do yours."

"I'm trying." After a deep breath, I updated Destiny on my morning activities. The meth word seemed to throw her, but not for long.

"The mothers' pasts are irrelevant. All that matters is whether they've been good mothers to Kayla. Have they?"

"I can't tell for sure. I haven't even met with Gwen."

"Does anything indicate otherwise? Is there something you're not telling me?"

"Like what?"

"Do you suspect that one or both of them had a part in this?"

"Not necessarily."

"Then that means someone abducted their daughter. I want you to call this woman. Can you write this down?"

"Hold on." I reached into my laptop case.

"Julianne Eaton. Here's her number."

Destiny rattled off ten digits, and I scribbled them on the back of one of my business cards. "Who is she?"

"A stay-at-home mom who tracks registered sex offenders. I need you to meet with her right away and work that angle."

"Work that angle?"

"You know what I mean."

"Shouldn't the police be pursuing this type of lead?"

"I told you yesterday," she said, sounding impatient. "Hillary thinks the lead detective has narrowed his focus to Gwen and Tracey."

"What about the stuffed animal searchers found? Have they verified that it belongs to Kayla? Tracey swears it does. She'd mended the leg—"

"It wouldn't matter, Kris. Gwen or Tracey could have planted it on the median. They knew people would be out searching on Sunday."

"You think they did?"

"No, but apparently the police do. I don't want them, the media or the public coming after Gwen and Tracey because they're lesbians. They shouldn't be railroaded or treated differently because of their sexuality."

Her fervor was beginning to alarm me. "I'm not sure it's a good idea to draw attention to Gwen and Tracey right now."

"The story's leading the local news every night, and it's on the front page of the morning papers. How many media classes have I taken? Nine," Destiny answered hotly before I could. "Whether we draw attention, or the police and protestors do, more is coming. Once a perception is cemented in the public's mind, it's almost impossible to alter. I'd rather control the information flow than try to play catch-up. I intend to reinforce the image of a strong, loving lesbian couple who are facing every parent's worst nightmare."

"This might not be the right couple to hold up as an example."

"Kris, please don't debate me. Just meet with Julianne. She's waiting for your call."

"Fine," I said, my tone conveying the opposite.

"Thanks. I've got to go now. I have to work out details of the tip line and reward before the press conference this afternoon."

"You're holding a press conference today? In addition to the vigil?"

"At four o'clock. Hopefully, it'll be the lead story on the early news, and then they'll splice in footage from the vigil for the ten o'clock broadcasts. The images will be perfect."

"I don't know," I said tentatively.

"Trust me, Kris. I know what I'm doing. And promise me, no more fights with the protestors."

"All right," I muttered.

"I'll be at the house before three. I'll see you—" she said, stopping mid-sentence. "What's that noise?"

I shook my head in amazement. "Five motorcycles just drove by in formation."

"I forgot to tell you," Destiny said sweetly. "Fran called in the Pride Riders."

• • •

"You realize, I assume, that there's a high probability Kayla Martin was abducted for the purpose of sexual abuse."

"It's possible, but—" I started.

"You also understand, I hope, that strangers who murder children typically kill their victims within three hours of the abduction."

I looked away from the gym floor, where three- and four-year olds in bright leotards were performing rolls, cartwheels and handstands. "Why are you telling me this?" I said to Julianne Eaton.

The forty-something, gaunt woman with wild hair looked less like a sexual abuse activist and more like a harried mother of four. She had on a food-stained T-shirt and skin-tight workout pants, and she spoke at a rapid-fire pace with a slight lisp.

At her request, we were meeting on the top row of bleachers inside the Prairie Recreation Center in Thornton, a northern suburb of Denver. Julianne was multitasking, hands flying across the keyboard, while her four-year-old daughter practiced on a beam apparatus that had been lowered to the floor. The other children were spread out among scaled-down uneven bars, vaults, triangular rings and trampolines.

"To prepare you." Julianne gestured at her laptop. "I did some preliminary checking. A dozen convicted sexual felons live within walking distance of Kayla's home. Thirty-four live in Highlands Ranch. I can try to entice one of them into dialogue with me, but as I mentioned to Destiny, this isn't my specialty."

"What is?"

"Catching sexual predators who prey on adolescent girls."

My eyebrows shot up. "How'd you get into that?"

"Two years ago, I caught my thirteen-year-old daughter walking to an IHOP to meet a thirty-four-year-old man she'd been chatting with on the Internet," Julianne said casually. "I put her in counseling and made it my mission to protect other vulnerable children."

"Have you had any success?"

"Quite a lot, actually. I send the intelligence I've gathered on predators to local authorities, and in the past year, I've handed over more than two hundred packets of information. Forty-two predators have been arrested."

"All men?"

"Yes, but to be fair, they're the only ones I target in chat rooms."

"How do you catch them?"

"I've adopted the language and tastes of my daughter and her friends, and I'm rather convincing. I use teenage colloquialisms and shorthand, and I've also become conversant in the lingo of predators. I have twenty or thirty online identities going at any given time, and I'm a patient woman." Julianne paused to clap and wave at her daughter. "As I'm developing the relationships, I make educated guesses as to who's behind the screen identities and what their intentions might be. With practice, it's become second nature. These aren't master criminals. For the most part, the ones I've caught have been what you would otherwise consider decent men. Members of society who pass as quote-unquote normal, but who live shadow lives that are destroying the lives of young girls. These are terrifying times we live in. We all have to be vigilant."

"Is it likely that by going online, you could find whoever took Kayla?"

"Frankly, no. But I might be able to entice someone who knows the abductor into exchanging e-mails with me."

A whistle blew, and all of the children completed their routines and ran to the large mat in the middle of the room. "This sounds like trying to find a needle in a haystack."

"With an estimated eight thousand registered sexual offenders in Colorado and six hundred thousand spread across the U.S., it is."

"Those numbers, I assume, don't include the ones who haven't been caught and convicted."

"Correct," Julianne said, nodding. "But just as technology has contributed to the ease of sexual abuse, it's also offered us solutions. Within seconds of notification of an abduction, law enforcement personnel can pull up names and addresses of all registered sexual offenders in the area. Some agencies, if they have the right software, can also retrieve names and addresses of family members and known associates of offenders, and map everything within a three-mile radius."

I glanced across the room and watched as a row of little girls posed with their arms outstretched, chests forward, smiles plastered on their faces. "The Highlands Ranch police have done that?"

"I would hope so."

"Yet, they haven't named any suspects, much less made an arrest."

"No, but that may be because they're missing the most vital piece of the puzzle, which is offenders who've failed to register who might be living or working nearby. The ones flying under the radar are the most likely to re-offend. Last month, I met an ex-FBI agent online who's developed a sophisticated software program that can interface with other data retrieval programs. After I talked to Destiny this morning, I sent Freddie Sampson an e-mail, and she's agreed to help. Sometime in the next few days, she should be able to send us a list of potential suspects."

I let out a groan. "Days?"

Julianne nodded. "I'm sorry it can't be sooner. The data crunching is the easy part. After that, vast amounts of information need to be compiled and evaluated by a trained professional."

"Freddie's search will be more comprehensive than the HRPD's?"

"Much. She'll find sex offenders who might be living in Highlands Ranch but haven't registered. She'll find others who registered and moved. She'll include sex offenders who work in the area. She'll search the registries of all fifty states and access convictions that predate offender registration laws. When the police search for sex offenders, typically, they come up with too many prospects and waste a lot of time knocking on doors. That approach falls short when the victim might still be alive."

"What does Freddie do that's so different from the way the police would approach this?"

"She takes her information and cross-references it to social security traces, work histories, credit applications, personal profile pages in social networking sites, anything she can find on the Internet. She then uses her experience and intuition to add or eliminate suspects. She'll give us a handful of profiles, at the most, complete with photographs, known aliases and thumbnail sketches of their past convictions and current lifestyles."

"But none of this will help capture the person who abducted Kayla if that person was never charged with a sexual crime?"

She smiled grimly. "No."

I glanced at the giant clock on the gymnasium wall. "There's nothing we can do but wait for Freddie to provide her report?"

"Other than inform parents at tomorrow night's meeting and try to prevent future abductions? No."

My eyes narrowed. "What meeting?"

"Didn't Destiny tell you?" Julianne said offhandedly. "At my suggestion, she's called all of the homeowners' associations in Highlands Ranch and invited them to a community meeting at the Meadowridge clubhouse."

CHAPTER 7

When I returned to Highlands Ranch, Pine Lane was crammed with motorcycles, satellite news trucks, church vans and a police cruiser. I was forced to park on Spruce Drive and walk the short distance to the Martin-Reid home.

At the bottom of the driveway, I cut past five motorcycle riders in full leather and approached Fran, who was unloading boxes from the back of her purple Ford Ranger.

"Destiny is *not* the boss of me," I tossed out as my opening remark.

Fran paused to push her sunglasses to the top of her crew cut. "She riding herd on you again?"

"What's that supposed to mean? *Again.*"

"Give me a hand with the last of this cargo, would you?" she said, thrusting a carton full of Tupperware in my direction. "Your honey knows how to get things done. That's a fact."

"Not at home. I'm still waiting for her to finish the caulking job she started on the tub last winter."

Fran chuckled and hung a fruit basket on my wrist. "Different circumstances. Let her think she's in charge on this. You and me, we'll do whatever we choose. Same as always."

"I just drove up to Thornton to meet with a stay-at-home mom who calls herself a sexual abuse activist."

"What's she got to do with the case?"

"I heard ten different ways Kayla could have been molested by now."

Fran grimaced. "Not a positive attitude."

"I feel like taking a bath."

"How's this affect us?"

"That's my point. Destiny knows we intend to interview friends and family, people who know Kayla, Gwen or Tracey. Why did she make me meet Julianne Eaton?"

"Might have wanted to pre-qualify her. Didn't have time herself. Sent you instead."

"Pre-qualify her for what?"

"This Julianne part of Destiny's public campaign?"

"Apparently. The two of them have invited all of the homeowners' associations in Highlands Ranch to a meeting tomorrow night."

Fran shook her head. "Not sure what your girlfriend's up to. You'd better find out tonight, when you two're spooning between the sheets."

I rolled my eyes and glanced down at my arms. "What is all of this?"

"Food and gifts for Gwen and Tracey. Fraction of what was dropped off at the Lesbian Community Center. Destiny's bringing another load when she comes this afternoon."

"Where are we putting it?"

She grabbed a deli platter and fruit plate from the front seat of the truck. "Nonperishables, kitchen island. Gifts and cards, dining room table. Anything that needs cooling, fridge in the garage."

"Is Gwen back yet?"

"Just got home. Holed up in the master suite." Fran winked at someone behind me, and I turned in time to see a woman in a sleeveless leather vest, black sports bra and silver lace-up boots tender a slight wave.

I snapped my fingers to get Fran's full attention. "Where's Tracey?"

"Basement rec room. Stereo on, full blast."

We turned and walked side by side into the two-car garage. "Who put the yellow caution tape around the yard?"

"Yours truly. Needed to set some boundaries for the Christ freaks. Still," Fran said, flashing a lecherous grin, "that white-haired lady in the pillbox hat's kind of cute. Could do without that baritone boomer on the crate, though. Voice like a megaphone." Fran opened the refrigerator and almost knocked over a mountain bike with the door. "Nothing'll fit in here. Better take out the soda."

I set my items on the spotless concrete floor and began to pull out cartons of Pepsi, Sprite and bottled water. "How can you be so calm?"

"Thirty years in the convent taught me a thing or two. Don't let them infuse hatred into you, kiddo."

"Why isn't it against the law to verbally assault someone?"

"Just ain't. Amazing how firmly committed they are to their way of seeing things," she said, almost admiringly. "Wonder where they got those outfits. Haven't seen cuts and colors like that since the Sixties."

"That sign, '*Homosexual parents are child abusers,*' doesn't bother you?"

"Not if I can understand where the sign-holder's coming from. Teen boy in the baby-blue suit holding it, right?"

"I didn't notice."

"Kid doesn't know any better. Following the doctrine laid down by his parents. Same one laid down by a mega-church minister, bet you. Kid can't help it if he's raised around Sacred Lifers. More like scared-to-deathers. Someday, he'll figure that out for himself."

"Maybe," I said doubtfully.

"Change of subject. Met with my cheerleaders on their lunch hour at Roosevelt High. Productive get-together." Fran pulled a spiral notebook from her back pocket and flipped it open. "Oh-eleven-hundred hours, interviewed Chelsey Bogan and the two females she roomed with at the Mountain Chalet in Vail. Brittany Stallworth and Megan Flood. Practiced simultaneous manipulation. Tidbit I learned in that seminar on interviewing techniques."

"Simultaneous manipulation?"

"All three at once," Fran said with a grin. "General consensus—the obscene photographs were snapped on Saturday morning, September eighth, between the hours of nine and eleven. While the aforementioned subjects were in a cheerleading clinic."

"Where was the camera?"

Fran scratched her head with the notebook. "Getting to that. Allegedly, Chelsey left the camera behind in the hotel room. Natural conclusion—someone must have come into the room, had a few jollies and left behind the perverse little gift."

"You're certain none of the three girls took the shots?"

"Said they didn't. Giving 'em the benefit of the doubt—for the moment. Leaves us with the females on the hotel staff and the females connected with Roosevelt High who came on the trip. One of them has to be our shutterbug."

"A guy could have taken the camera, snapped shots of a woman and brought it back."

"Dang. Never thought about that." Fran frowned. "Table that theory for now. Doesn't feel right. Feels more personal. Any-hoo, going to forego a meeting with the hotel staff, for the time being. Wouldn't mind a scenic drive to Vail on the client's tab, but too busy here in the Mile High City to break away. Focus on Roosevelters. One of our three roomies lent a key."

"One of them admitted that?"

"Heck no, but this ain't my first rodeo. Two questions into it, knew Miss Brittany Stallworth was lying. Cheeks turned red, voice sounded funny, broke eye contact. But stuck to her story. Tomorrow, plan to tail her from home to school. Drives herself every day, according to Chelsey. Catch B.S. in the parking lot alone. Give her a chance to come clean. Save me a lot of pavement-pounding if I can get a confession and narrow the list from forty-three females to one."

I gasped. "Forty-three?"

Fran nodded. "Same weekend the cheerleaders held their camp, so did the girls basketball team. Adds complexity. All together, we got thirty female students—rah-rahs and athletes—plus four coaches and nine mothers who accompanied the squad and team. They rode the bus together, ate together, stayed at the Chalet together."

"What if Brittany won't tell you the truth? You can't interview forty-three people right now. We need to focus on Kayla."

Fran put up a hand. "Don't go getting hysterical on me. Had a breakthrough earlier. Allowed me to eliminate the underage crowd."

"How?"

"See for yourself." She pulled a photograph from the back of the notebook and tried to hand it to me.

I pushed it away. "Eww. Not again. I've already looked at this."

"Not in good light." Fran steered me by the arm, out of the garage and into full sun. When I refused to touch the picture, she held it inches from my eyes. "Tell me that snatch, for all practical purposes, doesn't eliminate the teenage suspects."

Through the eye I'd left partially open, I saw Fran's point.

Strands of gray were nestled among the brown pubic hairs.

I found Gwen in the master bedroom, curled up in a chair in front of the bay window. Through a slit in the draperies, she seemed to be watching the street.

I moved a silk throw pillow to the king-size bed and sat down in the matching chair next to Gwen. On the round table between us, there was a stack of cards and e-mails. Noise from a flat-screen television mounted above the gas fireplace competed with cries from the protestors.

I touched Gwen on the shoulder, and she raised her head. "How are you doing?"

She smiled faintly. "Every day, I feel like this is the day."

I reached for the remote and hit the mute button, silencing the local news broadcast. "That you'll find Kayla?"

She nodded. "I get up in the morning, and I know I'll see her. Then night falls, and she's still out there, all alone somewhere, asking for her mommies. What's today?"

My stomach tightened. "Monday, September seventeenth."

"I can't keep track of the days. I never sleep for more than a few minutes at a time, and the middle of the night's the worst. I just shake with fear, not knowing where she is or what's happening to her. The first two days, I couldn't sleep at all. I closed my eyes, and all I could see was the terror on her face. I have to find her."

"Where did you go this morning?"

"Everywhere. Nowhere." She ran a hand through her hair, parting her bangs. "I have to get away from the phone. I'm afraid to answer it. I don't want to get the call that she's dead. Waiting is the worst part. The house is too quiet. I haven't been able to go into Kayla's bedroom since Thursday. I can't deal with not seeing her there. Tracey's been sleeping in her bed." Gwen paused to take a deep breath. "Tracey believes she's dead, you know."

I nodded. "She told me that. Do you?"

She sniffled and wiped the back of her hand across her nose. "I won't let myself go there. This morning, I passed out fliers to businesses along Ranch Boulevard, and I'm not looking for a body," she said defiantly. "I'm looking for my daughter. I don't want any more time to go by without her. I have to do everything I can to bring her back."

"I understand."

A long silence passed, before she added, "I'm not sure I've grasped this."

"I don't know how anyone could."

"I haven't cried yet. I'll probably fall apart later, but right now, that's not an option. I'm more worried about Tracey. She's the one who spends every day with Kayla, and she was here when . . ." She paused, shaking her head. "I can't imagine what this must be doing to her. All she ever wanted was to give Kayla a safe environment, the childhood she never had."

I raised an eyebrow. "Tracey had difficulties?"

"That's an understatement." Gwen put a hand to her cheek. "She was taken from her drug-addicted mother when she was ten months old and placed in foster care. After that, she was moved twelve times. Foster homes, group homes, two failed adoptions. She aged out of the system at eighteen and was homeless for a while."

I took a deep breath. "She never said anything to me."

"She doesn't like to talk about it. She got her GED, enrolled at Metro State and eventually trained to be a closed-captioner. She's one of the best in the country. Tracey can type two hundred and fifty words per minute, at ninety-nine percent accuracy," Gwen said in a flat tone.

"She joked that she watches TV for a living."

"She always downplays it, but she's covered presidential debates and Olympic events."

"That's impressive!"

"After Kayla was born, Tracey decided to work less hours so we wouldn't have to put Kayla in daycare. Now she does closed-captioning for DVDs. There isn't as much pressure, and she can set her own hours. She does most of her work after I get home or when Kayla's asleep."

I handed Gwen a sheet of paper with tiny writing on both sides. "I had Tracey make a list of everyone who might have come into contact with Kayla in the past few months. I asked for family members, and—"

She interrupted. "You won't see any of those."

"Not even on your side?"

Gwen limply reached for the sheet. "My family disowned me when I was sixteen. I've tried to get in touch several times since, including after Kayla was born, but they won't have anything to do with us."

"I asked Tracey to include neighbors, playmates, friends, acquaintances, co-workers, friends of friends, repairmen, delivery men, service providers. When you get a chance, could you look at what she's come up with and add to it, if possible?"

"I can't think straight right now."

"Tracey didn't know some of the people's last names, so whatever you could fill in would be helpful."

Gwen dropped the list into her lap. "I'll try."

"Thanks. Off the top of your head, can you think of anyone who showed a special interest in Kayla?"

"Everyone loves her. She's always smiling and giggling."

"Let me rephrase that—anyone with an unhealthy interest?"

Her face fell. "What kind of mothers do you think we are? We would never allow that."

"I didn't mean to imply anything," I said hastily.

"No one would want to hurt Kayla."

"Can you think of anyone who might want to hurt you or Tracey, to get back at you for something?"

"The police have asked me variations of that question every day. No!"

"Tracey mentioned Bruce McCarthy, Kayla's father."

"Sperm donor," Gwen corrected. "He wouldn't do this. He doesn't care enough to make the effort."

"What do you mean by that?"

"In February, we cut off his visitations because he was too inconsistent. It hurt Kayla's feelings when he canceled on her. Bruce always acted like he wanted to participate in her life, but if something better came along, he stood us up. We didn't need his negative influence, and we decided to enforce our original agreement."

"Which was no contact?"

"No contact."

"How did Bruce take that?"

"Like someone had revoked his gym membership," she said with scorn.

"Does Bruce have a key to your house?"

"He used to, but we asked for it back."

"Does anyone else?"

"Kim, next door."

"Sierra's mom?"

Gwen nodded. "She keeps a copy, in case we get locked out."

"Are there any keys hidden outside?"

"No."

"When was the last time you changed the locks?"

"When we moved in, three years ago." Gwen shuddered. "I can't believe this happened in Highlands Ranch. We moved away from downtown so Kayla would have a safe place to grow up and friends to play with."

"Please don't take offense at this, but do you believe everything Tracey's told you about what happened on Thursday?"

"Of course I do," she replied in a lifeless tone. "Why wouldn't I?"

"Tracey told me that she'd been addicted to meth. Is there any chance she had a relapse? Could she have been high that afternoon?"

Gwen began to tremble. "We'll never be free of it, will we?"

"Free of what?"

"Our pasts. They'll always interfere with our futures, no matter who we are or what we become."

"We?"

She looked me in the eye with an intensity that unnerved me. "If you're going to accuse Tracey of something, you'd better include me."

"I'm not sure I understand."

"She didn't tell you how we met?"

"No."

"In a rehab clinic," Gwen said bluntly. "I was addicted to meth, too."

CHAPTER 8

"Gwen Martin and Tracey Reid are two of the most loving mothers I know. They are exceptional parents who had their lives shattered last Thursday afternoon, when their three-year-old daughter Kayla went missing." Destiny raised her voice. "They've built their lives around Kayla, lives that have been destroyed by her abduction."

The flame of the candle in Destiny's hand brought a soft illumination to her face, and the scores of women in front of the Martin-Reid home seemed drawn to her every word.

Looking up at the canopy of stars and sliver of moon, I realized with a start that this would be the fifth night Kayla Martin would spend away from home. Eight o'clock. She'd now been missing for more than a hundred hours.

The Christian protestors had departed at dusk, and Fran had pulled down the stakes and yellow tape, allowing supporters to spill from the grass and driveway onto the sidewalk and street. Women stood silently, cradling candles, wiping away tears, holding hands and embracing.

Most who had arrived between nine and ten seemed to be strangers to Gwen and Tracey. Only a handful had approached the mothers to offer condolences, and none had lingered for long. Gwen had clasped each well-wisher in a full-body hug, while Tracey barely had touched anyone and had turned her head to the side with each clutch. From what I could determine, few neighbors were in attendance.

I stood next to the mailbox at the curb, near a makeshift shrine. The light of a streetlamp shone on colorful placards, signed cards, flower arrangements and rainbow flags. Votive candles and stuffed animals surrounded a two-foot-by-three-foot laminated photograph of Kayla. A child's crayon drawing of a little girl lay on the lawn, the words "I miss Kayla" scrawled across the bottom.

"We're here tonight," Destiny continued, "to honor Kayla, to bring attention to her disappearance and to support Gwen and Tracey in whatever way they need. Gwen would like to say a few words."

Gwen and Tracey rose from their folding chairs at the top of the sloped driveway. "We just want Kayla back. She's all we have," Gwen said, in essence repeating comments she'd made at the press conference held earlier at police headquarters.

Tracey hadn't spoken then, perhaps because she had virtually no voice left. The cracking I'd heard in the morning had disintegrated until it sounded like a forced, painful whisper. She'd sat rigid at four o'clock, next to Gwen, staring straight ahead, as if in a daze, unblinking against the lights of the news crews. At this moment, she appeared only slightly more comfortable and coherent. Like Gwen, she looked drawn and pale and was dry-eyed.

Gwen moved to sit down, and Destiny—appearing startled by the brevity of Gwen's remarks—added hurriedly, "Gwen and Tracey appreciate everything the community is doing on their behalf and Kayla's."

Gwen gave a feeble nod, and Tracey motioned listlessly.

"They've asked Maureen Calgary to lead us in a meditation."

A woman dressed in a white linen pantsuit, with black hair flowing down to her waist, suddenly appeared at Destiny's side. She raised her hands, palms up, and said in a soothing voice, "If you could take the hand of whoever's nearest you and hold it tight."

I felt someone grab my right hand and looked down to see Sierra Frazier, barefoot and in pink flannel pajamas. The nine-year-old smiled up at me.

"Where did you come from?" I whispered.

"Next door, silly." She scrunched up her face. "But don't tell my mom. I'm on restriction."

"What's restriction?"

"When you get in trouble and can't do things."

"What did you get in trouble for?"

"I wasn't supposed to go outside today or talk to anyone, since I was home sick, but I forgot."

"Sorry about that," I said, apologizing for my part in the transgression her mother had caught on the webcam. "Does your mom know you're here now?"

"No. She's in bed. She drinks a lot. I'm not supposed to leave the yard," Sierra said, eyeing the property line ten feet away.

"I'll go stand over there with you."

"C'mon!" she said, tightening her grip on my fingers.

Sierra and I cut across the grass, still holding hands. I noticed the four policemen on the periphery of the crowd hadn't reached for human touch, nor had any members of the three news teams.

Maureen projected her voice. "Close your eyes and visualize Kayla's happiness and well-being." After a thirty-second pause, she added, "Visualize her safe return to the arms of Gwen and Tracey."

In the background, I began to hear the muffled sounds of sobbing.

"We're all connected. We're all family," Maureen intoned, swaying back and forth, as if in a trance. "Let us offer our love and kindness to these two mothers who are in pain. Don't merely support them in their grief and suffering. Share it with them so that they know they're not alone."

I felt a tug on my hand and opened my eyes to Sierra's wide-eyed gaze. "Where is Kayla?"

"I don't know. I wish I did."

"Is she coming back?"

"I hope so."

"My mom says she isn't and that I should stop talking about her."

Before I could reply, Maureen's alto interrupted. "Visualize comfort and serenity for Gwen and Tracey. Create a sacred space for them that transcends all evil. Picture them bathed in white light as they wait patiently for their loving reunion with Kayla. Let us take them in our arms, the three of them. Reconnect them as the loving family they were on Thursday morning, before they faced these challenges. Return them to a state of peace."

I had just begun to follow orders, adding to the group energy of changing an individual reality, when I heard a shrill voice call out, "Stay away from my daughter. You did enough damage this morning."

I opened my eyes in time to see a woman dragging Sierra away by the arm.

Evidently, Kim Frazier had recognized me from the Webcast.

An hour later, the same twinkling stars I'd been standing under in Highlands Ranch had faded away, all but obliterated by the lights of downtown Denver.

"Hold this for a sec, would you?" Fran handed me a mini Maglite, which I shined on the section where she groped.

"This is gross."

"No argument there. Might not want to step over here."

"Where?"

"Never mind."

I trained the narrow beam toward my feet. "I'm in it, aren't I?"

"Could be," Fran said with a broad smile.

"Sick! What is it?"

"Kitty litter. Used. Couple logs and *beaucoup* clumps. Some pussy needs Imodium."

I shook my foot. "What's the point of us paying exorbitant fees to information services, if we have to come out and do this?"

"Best of both worlds. Combine the virtual with the real, computer work with fieldwork. Can thank me and Salvation Army for the preparations," she said, gesturing at our outfits. "Twenty bucks for the lot."

Fran was wearing work boots, knee socks and a cap, and with the added flannel shirt and safety-orange pants, she looked like a hunter. In a ski mask and Lycra, I resembled a bank robber on my way to aerobics. Upon completion of the task, we planned to leave the clothes where we stood, in a Dumpster in the alley between Seventh and Eighth Avenues, off Grant Street.

The scent of fall might have been in the air, but all I could smell was the Vaseline I'd applied liberally to my upper lip. The greasy balm had mixed with sweat, making for an uncomfortable combination. I would have loved to have shed some layers, but Fran had advised—on a tip from a recent seminar—the heavier the clothes, the better. I'd complained mightily as we'd donned protective layers under the light of the lone streetlamp, especially annoyed with the latex gloves and hospital masks.

As I sifted through a garbage bag laced with raw eggs and cigarette butts, however, I was thankful for the extra layer of rubber afforded by the dishwashing gloves I'd thrown on at the last minute.

"Funny thing about trash," Fran observed as she straightened up and rubbed her lower back. "Some items are untouchable only after they've been used. Take Kleenex, Kotex or Trojans, for example."

My eyes, the only exposed part of me, telegraphed disgust. "Fran!"

"Others, only when deprived of refrigeration. Like milk or meat."

I stopped digging. "What's your point?"

"Or unpleasant in combination. Like chocolate syrup and white rice."

I stifled a laugh. "This isn't helping."

She shook her head mournfully. "By the looks of this mess, never know this generation's supposed to care about the environment. Free curbside recycling in Denver, and what've we got here?" She kicked at a pile. "Newspapers, empty bottles, cans. Not to mention wasted food. Cooked and uncooked. Should be consumed as fuel, waste products traveling past the property lines through the sewer pipes. But no, here it is, journeying above ground to the city landfill."

"Don't start!"

"Just saying. Can't blame people for discarding items such as French bread and bananas—completely unrealistic windows for consumption—but shame on people for everything else we're standing in."

"I have to ask again. Why are we here?"

Fran leaned against the side of the Dumpster, her elbows propped on the top metal bar, looking as relaxed as if she were poolside. "Because trash never lies, my friend. Whiskey bottle rats out a recovering alcoholic. Syringe snitches on an addict. Pregnancy test busts a wife who hasn't had sex with the hubby in years. Gay porn informs on a married minister. Inside this Dumpster lie the unedited stories of people's lives. Pretty thrilling stuff!"

"How much longer do we have to stay? Between the stench and the squish . . ." I stopped, unable to complete the sentence.

"Till we come across something with Bruce McCarthy's name on it or get to the bottom of the pile. Whichever comes first."

I groaned. "That'll take forever."

"Clean off your torch, and it'll go faster."

"Nah," I said, unwilling to retrieve my flashlight from the load of diapers where I'd last seen it.

"Got this down to a system," Fran said, demonstrating. "Hoist a bag. Rip it open. Rummage around for identifying paperwork. No luck? Toss the bag to the side. Grab another bag."

"You're sure this isn't illegal?"

"Trash's fair game once it crosses that line." Fran pointed to the fence that surrounded the mansion behind us. "Anyone can have it."

I sat on a computer box filled with Styrofoam. "I'm bored."

"Then scoot over here and help."

"No, thanks."

"Gimme the light."

I handed it to her and frowned at a green hunk of prime rib. "I'm never going to eat again."

"Trash seems worse when it belongs to someone else," Fran said mildly, between heaves. "Got to apply detachment to the project, or this job's one prolonged gag."

"What did you find out about Bruce McCarthy?"

"B.M.? Not much—"

"Don't call Kayla's father that when I'm standing in this."

She grinned and whispered loudly, "Brucie has lived here at Eighth and Grant for six years, in a piece of that twenty-thousand-square-foot castle that takes up half the block." She inclined her head toward the red sandstone building behind us. "Mansion was built with gold rush money in the early nineteen hundreds, split into fourteen condos in the Eighties. Developer did a nice job, what with the gated grounds and brick courtyard, don't you think?"

I shrugged. "I can't see much in the dark."

"It's a beaut. Our buddy Bruce owns a two-bedroom penthouse that faces the street. Drives a vintage Porsche. Works as a software engineer, same as Gwen. Independent contractor in the telecom industry. Good credit. No run-ins with Johnny Law. No ex-wives. Can't tell about ex-boyfriends. They might be coming and going, turnstile-fashion, for all I know. Not unfolding how we'd like."

"What do you mean?"

"Two meth mothers cut out Pops, who looks like an outstanding citizen."

"On paper."

"True enough. Have to see what the trash has to say. Do know Brucie likes to party hearty. Including Saturday night. Couldn't have been too broken up about his little girl's disappearance. Saw a picture of him at a sports bar near Coors Field."

"Where'd you find the photo?"

"On the 'Stealth Party' Web site."

"What's that?"

"Gay men's idea of a good time. B-Mac seems to be one of the main rabble-rousers. The boys spread the word through e-mail blasts, huddle up in groups of twenty or more and spring themselves on straight bars and nightclubs. No warning. Stealth attacks. Party for the night. Move on to a new locale the following weekend."

I rolled my eyes. "Why?"

"Beats me. All in good fun, if you consider mocking heteros fun."

"Hmm," I said, shifting my weight to get more comfortable. "I'm meeting him tomorrow at his office. That should be interesting."

"How'd you connect?"

"I told you earlier. Destiny set it up."

"Righto. What time?"

"Nine o'clock."

"You want company?"

"No. You're going to hang out at the park by Kayla's house to see if the weird guy Tracey saw shows up. Remember? Did we even have this conversation, right before the vigil started?"

"Suppose we did. At the time, might have been a tad distracted by the woman in the net shirt. Sorry about the slip."

"What if Bruce uses a shredder? This'll be a complete waste of time."

"Not necessarily. The smart ones turn the bills and credit card offers into confetti, but no one thinks to rip the junk mail and mag subscriptions into little pieces. All we have to do," Fran said, tucking the Maglite into her armpit, "is match a name to a trash bag, then search the lode." She reached deep into a white bag, pulled out a wad and shook liquid off the papers. "Hope that was tomato juice on the *Forbes* and *Robb Report*," she muttered, before letting out a satisfied cry. "Ah, ha! What do we have here?"

"You found him?"

"Him, and Kayla, too."

I bolted up and almost took a header. "Seriously?"

Fran put up her hand for a high five. "She's alive, Kris!"

CHAPTER 9

Fran's exultation, unfortunately, was premature.

In the bag of trash containing mailers addressed to Bruce McCarthy, she'd found a Captain Crunch cereal box and crayon stubs, items she was certain telegraphed Kayla's recent presence at his condo.

I wasn't so sure.

We climbed out of the Dumpster and crept down the alley, around the corner and into another alley. In a nook between two detached garages, we poured our finds onto a queen-size tarp Fran had fabricated out of construction-grade trash bags and duct tape. Using hand trowels to separate the useless from the useful, we cleaned the latter off as best we could. The good stuff, we placed in a fresh trash bag.

Before we left, we stripped down to the clothes we'd worn under the cover of Salvation. Fran exited the alley in high-waist jeans, T-shirt and orange Crocs. I left wearing low-rider jeans, a short-sleeve golf shirt and loafers.

On the short trip back to my house, we argued about whether real estate brochures for remote mountain property in the Northwest and ads for freelance engineer jobs in Seattle meant Bruce McCarthy had kidnapped his daughter and hidden her, intending to start a new life for the two of them in another state.

I didn't believe the evidence was nearly as damning as Fran thought it was, and I tried to explain this to her for the ninth time when she called six hours later.

She'd wrenched me out of a deep sleep, and for the first confusing seconds, I didn't know whether it was morning, noon or night.

"Rise up, sunshine," Fran blared in a voice that instantly centered me.

"Mmm." I stretched and let out a grunt.

"You awake?"

"More or less."

"Sleep good?"

"No."

"Still stink?"

"Probably." I rubbed my eyes. "That stuff we found in Bruce's trash last night, I don't think it necessarily means anything. I really don't."

"Table that for the moment. Got some exciting news. Had a breakthrough with Brittany."

I yawned. "The cheerleader?"

"Bingo. Meet me at the office when you're done with McArthur."

"McCarthy," I corrected automatically, to the sound of a dial tone.

I could have strangled Fran for waking me up at seven thirty, robbing me of the extra thirty minutes of slumber I could have enjoyed before the alarm rang.

Rest I desperately needed after having spent the night alone.

Destiny had elected to stay in Highlands Ranch with Gwen and Tracey, a decision I'd supported, but I'd missed her.

Without her lying next to me, I'd struggled through the night, unable to fall asleep for hours.

Thoughts kept running through my mind, fragments of all of the things I had to do once the sun came up. Not tasks such as drop off library books, pay bills, replace lightbulb on front porch—all of which needed to be done. More like obtain names of sex offenders from Julianne Eaton, learn more about meth, intervene before Destiny torpedoed her career.

Throughout the night, I'd moved from the bed to the couch and back to the bed again, with at least ten visits to the bathroom in between, to release phantom pee.

I debated trying to get back to sleep, but then threw off the bed covers, took a deep breath and dragged myself into the shower.

My hair hadn't quite dried by the time I met with Kayla's father, but I'd brushed it back, brushed my teeth and slapped on some deodorant and ChapStick.

Sufficient grooming.

Bruce McCarthy's office was located on the 16th Street mall, in the Clock Tower, a twenty-story historic landmark that dated back to 1903. Designed to emulate the bell tower of a Venetian cathedral, the downtown building once had stood adjacent to a department store that was razed in the late 1970s.

There were views in every direction from Bruce's lofty perch, which occupied the entire thirteenth floor. On this cloudless day, I could see a hundred miles of Rocky Mountains, as well as several prominent Denver skyscrapers.

The elevator door had opened into a marble entryway, and the focal point of the room was a five-foot tall antique safe that had been transformed into a bar. A square pillar in the middle of the space was covered in blond and brown zebrawood that matched the U-shaped work center dominating the area. Brightly colored rock concert posters from the Sixties were framed and mounted next to blueprints of the tower.

"I appreciate you meeting with me," I said as I rested my notebook on a leopard-print pillow on the red sofa where Bruce McCarthy had directed me.

Bald and in his fifties, Kayla's father had a broad chest, beefy biceps and watery blue eyes. He sat across from me in a low-profile, black leather chair, his feet propped up on the matching ottoman. "If it would help locate Kayla," he replied, "I would do anything in my power. Just think, as a parent, how I feel. I want to know what happened to my baby. If I could build a road out of tears, I'd walk on it until I found her."

"I'm sure this is difficult."

"You can't imagine how it's affected me. I've had to cancel a trip to Cancun. I'm exhausted. I can't eat. I can't sleep. I can't work," he said, taking a large swallow of orange juice. "I'm devastated. I feel like a part of me is missing. I've tried to reach Gwen, but she won't return my calls."

I could smell booze coming out of his pores, and I started to breathe through my mouth. "You're not on speaking terms with Gwen and Tracey?"

"Not at present."

"What happened?"

"Ask them," he said ruefully. "I've never been given a straight answer. One minute, I was in my daughter's life. The next, I wasn't."

"When did you last see Kayla?"

"Toward the end of January. She spent the weekend with me, and I brought her back a few hours late, but that wasn't unusual. My life's always in a state of flux. I can't predict when I'm going to be somewhere or what I'm going to be doing, which is why I had to cancel my February weekend with Kayla. A friend had a condo in Vail for the week, and I couldn't turn that down. When I called Gwen, she seemed fine with the change of plans, but I came home to a certified letter in my mailbox." He sneered. "I learned via postal delivery, thank you very much, that I was no longer welcome in my daughter's life. They stole my child and left me nothing. Now maybe they know how I feel."

"That sounds a little vindictive," I said in a mild tone.

"I didn't mean for it to come across as such, but what started out as a favor, almost a lark, turned into something much more. Neither of them seems to appreciate that."

"You're referring to your sperm donation?"

Bruce nodded. "As well as my subsequent contributions to Kayla's life. I'm not going to sit here and say I'm a perfect father. No one is. But I'm a damn good one. Her birth changed my life. I fell in love with her the moment I saw her. She has my ears and my eyes." He smiled, displaying a mouthful of veneers. "I remember visiting her in the intensive care nursery, when she was on an IV and hooked up to oxygen, just rocking her to sleep, thinking I'd never felt such unconditional love. She was so sweet and innocent. She used to pick flowers for me. Out of my flower pots." He let loose a little laugh, as if on cue. "She loved to dress up in princess outfits. For her last birthday, I bought her a tiara and three gowns, all pink. Pink was her favorite color, like the morning sun. She loved to get hugs and kisses from her dad. I would sing to her, made-up songs with ridiculous words, and she'd laugh until she was breathless. She made a magical sound that echoed through my life, even when I couldn't be with her," he said, his voice catching.

I shifted in my seat. "You talk about Kayla as if she's dead. Is that what you believe?"

"I don't know what to feel." Bruce paused, then added in a burst, "What if she is dead? I'll never see her blue eyes again, never feel her silky skin, touch her shiny hair, hold her little hand. I see little girls go by who remind me of Kayla, and I break down in tears."

"What do you think might have happened to your daughter?"

"I wish I knew." His eyes darted back and forth. "But if she's found, I'm going to sue for sole custody of her. I've consulted a lawyer who believes I have a good chance of winning. Despite the fact that Gwen and I signed an agreement before Kayla was born, our behavior didn't follow the pattern of those original intentions. I started as a donor, but I became a father. That gives me rights."

"When did you meet with a lawyer?"

"Yesterday. I would have done it earlier, but in the spring, I was busy with a project at work. This summer, I traveled every week. When the call came in Thursday, my priorities shifted instantaneously. Gwen and Tracey have lost my child. At best, that makes them careless and neglectful. Or . . ."

"They harmed Kayla themselves. Accidentally or on purpose?"

He raised one eyebrow. "Draw your own conclusions."

"Why don't you share yours with me?"

"There are a lot of holes in Tracey's story, don't you think? How could you not hear someone coming into your house unless you were passed out or strung out?"

I made a mark in my notebook, which seemed to please him. "Prior to this incident, would you have said Gwen and Tracey were good parents?"

"Gwen is."

"And Tracey?"

He tapped a finger on the arm of his chair. "She's controlling, and she thinks she's smarter than everyone else."

"How so?"

"She won't let Kayla play anywhere except that dingy room in the basement, and she keeps a baby gate up to prevent her from going upstairs. She doesn't want toys all over the house. Why? What would it matter? Tracey's too strict with Kayla."

"And Gwen?"

"Gwen's a good mother. She and I made a great team. We could have worked out our differences, if it weren't for Tracey."

"You believe Tracey came between you?"

"She must have. Gwen and I were friends long before Tracey came into her life. But Tracey has Gwen under her thumb."

"Did Kayla seem happy and healthy the last time you saw her?"

"I suppose." Bruce shrugged. "Except she was too skinny. Tracey said she was a picky eater, but she ate when she was with me. She loved Chicken McNuggets, and she always cleaned her plate. She looked sickly in January." He gazed out the window toward the mountains. "That last weekend, I braided her hair, and when I fell asleep on the couch, she slapped me to make me stop snoring. Why did this happen to me? My life will never be whole again."

"Don't give up."

"That's easier said than done."

"Have the police questioned you?"

"Twice, and I've offered to take a polygraph. I have nothing to hide. I haven't been in Highlands Ranch since January."

"You didn't care to join the search on Sunday?"

He ran his hands across his face. "It would have been awkward, seeing Gwen and Tracey under those circumstances. I'll return to Highlands Ranch only to take permanent custody of my daughter."

"I hope that's soon."

"I don't know." Bruce drew himself up with effort. "The police ought to be checking into Tracey's past. I told them that last week, and I haven't seen anything in the news about it."

I shut my notebook and rose. "I assume you're referring to her drug addiction."

"Actually, I was referring to the double life she led before she met Gwen," he said casually. "I wonder if anyone's interviewed Shelby Valentine about Tracey's thieving. That would be an interesting conversation."

CHAPTER 10

"By sheer coincidence, Bruce McCarthy met one of Tracey Martin's ex-lovers at a cast party in June," I said to Fran twenty minutes later, back at our office.

Fran paused in her study of the remotes she held in each hand, stared at me and raised one eyebrow. "You don't say?"

"Shelby Valentine. Have you finished the background check on her?"

"Right here." Fran tapped a folder on my desk. "But it ain't that illuminating."

"Shelby told Bruce that Tracey stole all of her money and walked out of her life five years ago."

"That explains the ex's poor credit scores." Fran sucked her teeth. "Shell-shocked press charges?"

"I hope not. Could you track her down and try to interview her today?"

"Will do. This a higher priority than catching the perv in the park?"

"Yes," I said, nixing our original plan. "You wasted three hours down there yesterday, on what's probably a wild goose chase."

"Not a complete waste of time. Used my laptop and cell to track down the carpet cleaner who showed up at the neighbor's on Thursday. Eliminated her as a suspect. Gal's worked for the company twelve years. Model employee. Course that query only took five minutes. Rest of the time was squandered."

"Let's wait until we hear from Julianne Eaton before you do any more stakeouts. Once she gets the sex offender profiles from her FBI friend and sends us photographs, we can show them to Tracey. If one of the men looks familiar to her—because she saw him in the park or somewhere else—we can try to track him down."

"When's the agent's report due in?"

"Supposedly any minute."

"Fair enough. Guess all we can do is wait."

I rubbed my forehead. "This does feel personal, though, doesn't it? Kayla's disappearance?"

"Couldn't agree more. You putting the disgruntled dad in the frame?"

"I don't know. I had trouble getting a read on him. He seemed oddly attached to Kayla in some ways and completely uncaring in others. If I had to guess, though, I'd say he didn't kidnap her. Full-time parenting would put too much of a crimp in his lifestyle."

"What about Daddy took her on Thursday, meant to keep her for a few days, but something went wrong? Accidentally killed her, had to dispose of the body? You like that scenario?"

I shook my head. "Why Thursday?"

"Why not? Good a day as any."

I winced. "Bruce couldn't have known Tracey would be napping when he arrived. It's too coincidental."

"Lay this on your brain. Brucie comes to visit, maybe to confront. Rings the bell. No answer. Goes around back. Enters through the sliding glass door. Sees Tracey zonked out in the master. Surprises Kayla. Tells her to be quiet. They're going on an adventure. She's happy to see her daddy. They sneak out the back, and off they go."

"To where? Why?"

"That's where the picture darkens," Fran said solemnly. "Where was Papa on Thursday afternoon?"

"He says he was working at his office."

"Anyone verify that?"

"I didn't check. I came straight here after I finished interviewing him."

"Let's assume the fuzz are working that angle. Let it go for now. Bruce-man say anything about moving out of state?"

"No, and there wasn't a way for me to tactfully broach the subject."

"Dang." Fran pinched her lower lip. "Can't eliminate Brucie as a suspect, but let's not pursue him either. Sound good?"

"Fine."

"Makes sense. Appreciate the emphasis on efficiency. Don't know about this new tact, though. Investigating one of the mothers. Destiny won't cotton to it. We bring her in the loop, or no?"

"Not yet."

"This line of inquiry bring us any closer to finding Kayla's abductor?"

"It could, but Destiny won't see it that way."

"All-righty then. Mum's the word."

I leaned back in my chair and let out a sigh. "So tell me about Brittany. Did you squeeze the truth out of her?"

Fran grinned. "Did I ever. Give you the dirt in a minute. First, you gotta get a load of this." She gestured toward the screen of the compact television she'd purchased for her afternoon soaps addiction.

"What is it?"

"Appearance on the morning news show. Taped it two hours ago. Brace yourself."

The head of a woman with dark circles under her eyes, sagging skin and loose, gray curls filled the screen.

"Just send me an eyeball," she said, her eyes dry and her tone sharp. "Send me a knee. Send me an ankle. Send me something."

I leaned forward. "Who the hell is that?"

Fran hit pause. "Dara Martin. Gwen's mother. Kayla's grand-mother. Lives in eastern Kansas."

"She came to Denver?"

"No, ma'am. An affiliate station in Kansas City interviewed her live this a.m. Catch this."

Fran pushed play, and in response to the reporter's question about when she'd last seen her daughter, Dara replied, "Not since she was sixteen. Gwen told us she was a homosexual, and that was that."

"She ran away from home?" the reporter asked.

"We asked her to leave. For the good of the family. We had younger children to consider. They were at an impressionable age."

"You weren't supportive of your daughter's lifestyle?"

"We didn't condone her choices, not by any means, but we made it a point not to be hateful. As I recall, the family was civil and tolerant."

"You never met your granddaughter Kayla?"

"No, and I didn't want to. It would have broken my heart to see the poor thing living under such trying circumstances. That's no way to raise a child. It's not natural."

"What would you imagine Gwen and her life partner Tracey are going through right now, as they await news of Kayla's fate?"

"I've never met this Tracey person they're talking about on the news, so I couldn't say."

"What about your daughter?"

"I'm sure my Gwen's staying in control. She's a very neat person. Very organized and clean, just like we taught her. She likes to fix things around the house. Her father passed those skills on to her. She's very intelligent in that way, knows as much as any man." Dara Martin paused, before adding deliberately, "Gwen never struck any-one. She grew up with three rough-and-tumble brothers, and she was in control of herself at all times. I don't know this person. This isn't the daughter I raised."

Fran clicked off the television, and I stared at her numbly. "What if Gwen saw that? She has the TV on constantly."

Fran blew air out her cheeks. "Better hope she was pounding the pavement when this vote of no-confidence aired."

"Moving on," Fran said, after returning from an extended bathroom break. She reached into her top drawer, whipped out a photograph and tossed it onto my desk. "Guess who that is."

I glimpsed at the picture, but didn't bother with a second glance. "I'm not in the mood to play identify the genitalia."

"You're no fun." She retrieved the photo and held it up. "Kristin Ashe, meet Jasmine Smith."

I pushed Fran's arm away from me. "Who is she?"

"English teacher at Roosevelt High. Also happens to coach the girls basketball team. Was on the same trip as the cheerleaders."

I groaned. "What's her relationship with Chelsey?"

"Smith doesn't know Chelsey."

"Then how did a photo of her end up in Chelsey's camera?"

"Classic case of mistaken identity," Fran said, deepening her voice to a mystery theater level.

I frowned. "Jasmine Smith meant to leave the picture for someone else?"

"Indeed," Fran said dramatically, before reverting to her normal tone. "Brittany was supposed to get the little gift. She shared a room with Chelsey in Vail, you know."

"Mmm."

"On Saturday, when Brittany was in her morning cheerleading clinic, Smith approached and asked to borrow her hotel key."

"Which Brittany gave her?"

"Yep. Smith said she wanted to leave a surprise for Brittany in her room."

"That's surprising all right," I said, casting an eye on the photograph Fran had placed on the desk, face-up.

"Brittany came back later in the day, didn't find anything, figured

Smith must have changed her mind. Didn't say anything to her or anyone else until I cracked her story this morning. Brittany's backpack's yellow. Same with Chelsey's." Fran paused, seemingly for effect. "Excepting that Brittany had her pack with her at the clinic."

"While Chelsey left hers in the room?"

Fran nodded. "Smith snuck in, took out the camera, snapped the photo of her—"

"Okay, okay." I put up a hand.

"And left without being seen."

"Until Chelsey looked at her photos."

"Yep."

"I take it Brittany knows Ms. Smith."

"Oh, yeah," she said, her voice lilting.

"How well? Has Ms. Smith harassed her?"

Fran's nose crinkled. "More like the other way around. Britt has a crush, big-time. Ask me, they're doing the nasty."

"What makes you think that?"

"Brittany swore Smith hadn't touched her, but maybe she touched Smith." Fran flashed a wicked smile. "Touch of oral servicing?"

"Fran, please!"

She turned somber. "Brittany begged me not to rat her out. Doesn't want Jazz getting in trouble."

I froze. "Jazz?"

"Gets worse. Brittany thinks the relationship's her fault. Says Jazz never felt this way about anyone. Kid's under the illusion she started it."

"Started what?"

Fran stood, pulled an apple out of the side pocket of her camouflage pants and tossed it from hand to hand. "Their special friendship, as she calls it."

I covered my eyes. "Ugh."

"Last year, Brittany took Ms. Smith's poetry class and kept coming in for extra help she didn't need, if you follow."

"Perfectly."

"This semester, smitten kid plans her day around bumping into her favorite teacher in the halls." Fran began to pace, in a state of excitement. "Practiced all summer so she could try out for the cheerleading squad and attend the girls basketball games. Doesn't even like cheerleading. Girl's behaving like a stalker."

I drew a long breath. "She's a senior, with a crush on her teacher."

"Junior, and it's more than that." Fran took a giant bite from the apple. "Thinks about Smith all the time. Thinks she's going to live with Teach soon as she turns eighteen."

I exhaled loudly. "I take it Brittany's parents don't know about her feelings for Jasmine Smith?"

"No, siree." Fran glowered as she chewed. "Nor do her friends. Doesn't hang out with them anymore. Afraid someone'll find out and tell on her. Only one who knows about this debacle is me. First off, Britt wouldn't unzip the lips. Then, wouldn't stop yapping."

"How did you get her to open up?"

Fran tossed the half-eaten fruit at the trash can five feet away and missed. "Acted like I had a crush on a camp counselor when I was her age. Every time I shared a secret, she forked over two."

"What're you going to do? Talk to Brittany's parents? Talk to the principal?"

"No," Fran said thoughtfully. "Need corroboration. Moment I report this to school officials, they'll be required to investigate. Can't brand the woman for life if the allegations aren't true. Rumors'll follow her to the grave. Better be damn sure before I destroy a career and a marriage."

"Jasmine Smith's married?"

"With a newborn." Fran cut across the room, picked up the apple from the floor and dropped it into the trash. "Ain't you gonna ask if it's a boy or a girl?"

I felt sick to my stomach. "No."

"Girl." Fran rose to her full height. "*If* Brittany Stallworth and Jasmine Smith are doing something, it's wrong, right?"

"Of course it is! Why would you ask something like that?"

"Teachers, camp counselors, troop leaders—object of every girl's crush. Every lesbian's fantasy."

"That doesn't make it right."

"Sure we shouldn't drop this? Given our greater concerns, Kayla's well-being and all?"

I studied her closely, noting that her cheeks had turned bright red. "You've lost it!"

Fran shrugged. "What if Brittany wants it, gets down on her knees and begs for it?"

"Underage teens can't legally give consent," I said with passion. "That's why sexual misconduct laws are in place. To protect vulnerable girls, especially from adults who are in a position of trust."

"Position of distrust," Fran mumbled, looking away. "Never thought about it like that."

CHAPTER 11

What the hell was wrong with Fran Green?

I didn't have time to find out.

By Fran's labored breathing and reluctance to make eye contact, I knew she was upset, but she wouldn't talk about her feelings. She said that she'd conduct a background check on Jasmine Smith, that I shouldn't worry about her, and that we needed to leave it at that.

Which I did.

I gathered everything I would need for the day and left for Highlands Ranch.

On Pine Lane, I found the number of protestors outside Kayla Martin's house had doubled from the day before. Fortunately, the man with the projection-voice was nowhere to be seen or heard, and no one else was shouting. The Christians marched in line for Mass, silently waved their toxic signs or rested on the lawn across the street from Kayla's.

Two police officers were stationed at the foot of the driveway, and I wondered whether they had been sent to keep peace with the protestors or to keep an eye on Gwen and Tracey.

Tracey answered the door on the third bell ring, opening it a crack. I slipped through, careful to avoid the tiny slip-on shoes on the mat.

"Good morning."

"You're still not feeling any better?"

She tugged at plaid pajama bottoms and a men's undershirt and answered in a groggy, fractured voice. "I'm so stuffed up, I can't breathe."

"Have you seen a doctor?"

"What good would that do?"

"You could get antibiotics."

"Why bother? I wouldn't take them."

I followed Tracey into the great room. "I didn't see Gwen's car out front."

"She must be gone."

"Where?"

"I don't know."

"Looking for Kayla?"

Tracey shrugged. "I guess."

"When did she leave?"

"I don't know. I was asleep in Kayla's room." She flashed an embarrassed look. "We're not sleeping together."

"Since when?"

"Thursday night."

"Is anyone here with you?"

Tracey shook her head. "I don't think so. Destiny must have left. She slept in the guest bedroom," she added, as if she owed me an explanation. "What time is it?"

I glanced at my watch. "Almost eleven thirty."

"I can't believe I slept that long."

"Did you take any medicine?"

"I wouldn't," she said defensively. "Not after what happened. I was up until five o'clock this morning. Every time I tried to sleep, my mind kept replaying Thursday."

"Did anything new come to mind?"

She pressed a tissue against the end of her nose. "Not really. Right after the police came to the house, they asked me where Kayla might have gone, where they should search. I told them the Fraziers' yard because that's as far as I thought she'd walk. That's the only place we let her go on her own. What else was I supposed to say? I told them Kayla wouldn't have left the house by herself, but they acted like they didn't believe me. Someone must have come inside and taken her. Someone she knew. She wouldn't have left the house with a stranger, not without crying. I would have heard her, wouldn't I have?"

"Let's sit down somewhere," I said, alarmed by the shaking of her limbs.

She cast a furtive look toward the front yard and street. "I can't stay up here. Not by those people."

"Where do you want to go? The basement?"

She nodded. "Can I get you something? A drink? A sandwich? We have so much food I don't know what to do with it all."

"No, thanks," I said, as I steered her by the arm, toward the stairway. "Have you eaten anything?"

"I can't. It hurts too much to swallow."

"You have to eat. You need to keep up your strength."

"I can't."

We cut through the kitchen to the stairs, and Tracey held on to the rail as she took each step. At the bottom of the stairs, she led us down a narrow hallway and into a room that was surprisingly bright. The painted yellow space had sun streaming in from four windows and was filled with Kayla's belongings. There was a dollhouse, an overflowing toy box, a small table and chairs, a child-size rocker and built-in shelves full of puzzles and books.

"This is horrible," Tracey said as soon we'd settled into green bean bag chairs. "Our lives have been turned inside out."

"You shouldn't pay attention to the media coverage. Reporters are paid to—"

"How can I not?" Tracey interrupted wearily. "Gwen has the TV or radio on constantly when she's home, and she reads the papers and tells me what people are saying. Every day gets harder. Between the waiting and the accusations . . ." Her voice gave out, and she took a sip of water from a bottle she'd picked up from the floor. "All I ever wanted was to give Kayla a safe home, and I couldn't even manage that."

"It's not your fault."

"I wanted to give her a normal life."

"You did. You are. You will."

"I never felt like I mattered to anyone. Kayla must feel like that now. She must be wondering why I've abandoned her."

"She's young. She'll recover from this. With love and support from you and Gwen, she'll get past it."

"What if she's dead? What if I let her down?"

"You didn't. There's no way to protect a child every minute of every day—"

"I didn't have a childhood. That's all I wanted to give her. A childhood."

"Gwen told me you grew up in foster care."

Tracey answered with a ragged smile. "I thought I was tough, that I could survive anything, but this . . ."

"You have to hold yourself together. Be strong, for Kayla's sake."

"Strong?" She let out a derisive sound. "I left foster care as soon as I could, when I was eighteen. The only one I could count on was myself. I lived on the streets for two years. I didn't have a high school diploma, but I kept finding jobs at coffee shops on Colfax. I didn't stay anywhere long. I would fight with people and get fired or quit. I slept below bridges, in alleys, on heating grates by the Capitol. I used to wear torn jeans and a leather jacket with screws sticking out of it, thousands of them. I had safety pins in my cheeks, piercings and tattoos everywhere. I was convinced I was going to die before I turned twenty, and I didn't care. I was into punk rock, and I was a violent, aggressive person. I'd pick fights with anyone. Mean bitches, men twice my size. My nickname was Psycho Tracey. I didn't take shit from anyone."

"What made you turn your life around?"

Tracey took a deep breath and let it out slowly. "One day, I wrote in my journal, 'Quit fucking yourself,' and I never raised my fist again. I enrolled in some classes at Metro, made the Dean's list, started to feel good about myself. I still wasn't sober, though. I had this friend, Marla, and we'd get together every Saturday night and drink a gallon of wine and black out. I had the most intellectual, stimulating conversations with her," she said with a wry smile. "Marla's the one who introduced me to meth. Life was bland when I was clean, but it was spectacular when I was high. I chased the moment and pissed away everything for that feeling. I was addicted for four worthless years."

"Until you went into rehab?"

She nodded and sniffed. "Which is where I met Gwen. That's when my life started. I was born for the first time when I was twenty-two years old. I was thinking about that last week, right before all this happened. How my life was finally settled. That I'd had years in a row of sobriety and contentment. That I could live, not necessarily happily ever after, but a life without pain every day. That I had created the family I'd never had. Gwen, Kayla and me. I'd found my peace in the world." Tracey stopped abruptly, cut short by a ringing sound.

I pulled my cell phone out of my pocket and took a quick look at the screen. "It's Destiny."

"Go ahead."

I flipped open the phone. "Hey."

"I have some awful news," Destiny said. "Are you sitting down?"

"Yes."

"Are you alone?"

"No," I said, trying to control my tone.

"Is Gwen or Tracey there?"

"Tracey is."

"Can she hear you?"

"Mmm."

"Go into another room."

"Now?"

"Quickly."

"What's wrong?" I whispered, from the powder room on the main floor, after I'd excused myself from Tracey.

"The police are holding a press conference in ten minutes, at noon."

My heart began to race. "Have they found Kayla?"

"No, but they found a storage locker belonging to Tracey."

"Where?"

"In northwest Denver. In it, there were fake IDs and other items used by ID theft rings."

"How do you know?"

"Hillary called a minute ago to give me a heads up."

"Shit! Are the police going to announce their findings?"

"Hillary's not sure. Can you watch the press conference and then talk to Gwen and Tracey?"

"All right."

"Call me back. I need to prepare a response to this."

"Okay."

"Just so you know, the police have also accessed Tracey's juvenile record."

I rubbed my forehead, practically abrading the skin. "Tracey has a record? For what?"

"Assault."

"As of ten o'clock this morning, we've called off the search for Kayla Martin and canceled the Amber Alert. We are no longer classifying this as a missing persons case."

I turned up the volume on the television in the great room and stood at the back of the room, transfixed.

Police Chief Seth Dunfey, of the Highlands Ranch Police Department, read from a script. "Since last Thursday, September thirteenth, when our department was notified about a possible abduction, we have made this case our number one priority. With the assistance of personnel from the Colorado Bureau of Investigation and detectives on loan from metro area police departments, we've conducted foot searches, aerial searches, underwater searches, canine searches and house-to-house inquiries. The scope of our investigation has involved up to eighty officers. The extra personnel have assisted us with follow-up interviews, reports and the execution of search warrants. We've completed more than sixty witness interviews. As of today, however, the officers who have been on loan are being reassigned back to their regular duties in their respective departments. They'll be available to assist again, if necessary, as developments occur."

I couldn't believe what I was hearing.

"This case remains a priority. We need to bring justice to this little girl, but we're shifting the focus of the investigation to the place where Kayla was last seen, in the eighty-nine hundred block of South Pine Lane. We'll start at her home and remain there until we're fully satisfied that we've looked at everything that might pertain to a crime. We will not be disclosing what type of evidence we find. We will not comment on whether anything from the house has been removed since our investigation began or will be removed."

I sprang up, dashed into the living room, looked out the window and stared in disbelief at the four police cars that had come to a stop at odd angles on the street.

In the background, I could hear the police chief's monotone. "We can't comment on specifics, but we're disappointed with the family for failing to fully cooperate. Gwen Martin and Tracey Reid hold the key to this investigation. We've made them aware of this, and they haven't been as forthcoming as we'd hoped. We're also concerned by the potential delay in reporting the disappearance. There's some discrepancy over when Kayla was last seen, which is of concern to us. We have a challenge understanding the time span between when she went missing and when she was reported missing on Thursday afternoon. Of greater concern is the information we've received from a source close to the family that Kayla Martin hadn't been seen in the days, or possibly weeks, leading up to September thirteenth. We believe this to be a credible tip. While we're trained not to judge people at the front end of an investigation, we do shift gears as soon as information becomes available. There have been certain inconsistencies in statements we've been given as they relate to the facts of this case."

I saw a red Nissan Altima weave through the patrol cars and screech to a halt in the driveway. Gwen jumped out of the car and came running into the house. She gestured angrily. "How can this be happening?"

I followed her into the great room "You know about the press conference?"

"I've been listening to it on the radio. What are they doing to Kayla?"

She froze in front of the television, tears pouring down her cheeks. I came up beside her and put my arm around her shoulders.

"Gwen Martin and Tracey Reid are persons of interest, and we'd like to formally interview them. Let me reiterate an important distinction. They are persons of interest. They are not suspects. The two women are free to go anywhere they like, but we will be keeping a close eye on them. At this juncture, we have no authority to put a hold on them. We would need probable cause to make an arrest, which we don't have. We have an extensive list of other people who also fall into the category of 'person of interest,' but some are of less interest to us than others. We can confirm that we have searched a separate location—outside of Highlands Ranch—but we cannot confirm whether anything was seized from that site or its possible connection to Kayla Martin's disappearance. A judge has sealed our search warrants, and we're barred from releasing any details."

"Does he know what he's saying?" Gwen choked out. "Does he know that he's just ruined our lives?"

I tightened my hold on her.

"Everything so far indicates that Kayla Martin was *not* abducted by a stranger, which should put the community at ease. We're at the stage now that most of our work will go on behind the scenes. It might not be transparent to the public, but we remain focused on finding Kayla and determining what happened to her. We're open to all possibilities, and we're not ruling out anything. From here forward, however, we won't be releasing any more information to the public unless a body turns up or an arrest warrant is issued."

Gwen broke free from my clutch, grabbed a glass off the end table and hurled it at the television screen.

I heard a gasp, turned around and saw Tracey fall to the floor.

CHAPTER 12

"We'll never get her back alive." Gwen twisted Kleenex between her shaking hands.

We'd helped Tracey up the stairs and into Kayla's room, where she'd insisted that she wanted to be left alone.

"Don't give up hope," I said, trying to block out Tracey's raw sobs, which could be heard from a floor away. "Remember the boy you told me about in Nebraska? The one who was found after four weeks? Or the girl in Pennsylvania who came home after ten months? Someone will recognize Kayla and call the tip line."

Gwen pressed her face against the bay window in the living room and shuddered. "Why aren't they coming inside?"

I followed her gaze to the four officers who had gathered in a circle near one of the patrol cars. "You should probably call a lawyer."

"We don't need a lawyer. We have nothing to hide."

"Just to be safe. If money's a problem, Destiny and I could—"

"Why are they questioning everything? They don't believe Tracey was really sick on Thursday? No one had seen Kayla recently? She had the crud, too. Why didn't we take her to the doctor? Because she has a chronic ear infection and has been on antibiotics three times in the past year. We didn't want to over-medicate her. Why is she so thin? Because she was born six weeks before her due date and was on oxygen for the first three months of her life. She's always been underweight, consistently in the thirtieth percentile. She's a picky eater. What are we supposed to do? Force food down her throat? They talk about her shyness. Why did she cling to me? Because she spends all day with Tracey, and when I come home, she's needy."

"Gwen, you can't listen to everything—"

"People are calling in to talk radio, questioning Tracey's parenting. Tracey and Kayla are in a Wednesday morning play group. You know what one of the mothers in that group told me last week? That Tracey's the most patient one, that they all wish they could be more like her. They've never heard her raise her voice. She never would have hurt Kayla. You have to believe that, Kris!"

"No one's saying—"

"They're questioning my commitment to my daughter. Why did I travel so much? They'd never be doing this if we were a straight couple. They're saying our house is immaculately clean, as if that's a bad thing. What do they think? That we murdered Kayla and then scrubbed away her blood? We don't have any of Kayla's pictures or drawings on our refrigerator. That's what one of the dads from Kayla's dance group told Channel Four. It's because magnets won't stick to stainless steel."

"Any minute, the police are going to walk through that door. You need to calm down—"

"Fuck the police!" Gwen shook with rage. "They asked me three times about bruises other people had seen on Kayla. I told them she's an active, energetic child. Kim Frazier was quoted in the paper today about the bruises. How dare she! Most of Kayla's injuries came after she spent time with Sierra. I told Tracey she shouldn't let them play together, that there's too much of an age difference, but Kayla adores Sierra."

"Did you ever say anything to Kim about Sierra's rough play?"

"No. We didn't want to make waves. We wanted to fit in," she said, letting out a hysterical laugh. "Fit in. The police are harping on whether Tracey told them that she'd last seen Kayla at one o'clock or four o'clock. She was in shock. She told the nine-one-one operator the wrong thing, but she corrected herself. Channel Nine news has a copy of the tape on their Web site. It's awful. How would you react if you woke up, and your daughter was gone? Would you want every word and emotion on the record, for everyone to hear?"

"I can't imagine—"

"The first night, one of the detectives commented on how Tracey's demeanor was flat and unaffected. She closed-captions in real time," Gwen said, her voice fading. "She's learned how to deal with stress. That's just how she is. I've never seen her cry before today. Not once. What are we going to do? How will we survive this?"

I simply stared at her, unable to construct an answer.

A few minutes later, in the hall, I answered my phone with a whisper. "Did you see that?"

"Those assholes are trying to convict Gwen and Tracey without an arrest or trial," Destiny replied. "Can you believe it?"

"It doesn't look good."

"How are they holding up?"

"Not well."

"Both of them watched?"

"Parts of it."

"Tell them not to worry. I'm preparing a response."

I went into the bathroom and closed the door. "A press release?"

"A press conference. This afternoon."

"Destiny, they're in no shape to address the media."

"They won't have to. I'll prepare a statement."

I grimaced. "You might not want to do that."

"What choice do we have? We need to shift the focus off Gwen and Tracey, back to Kayla. To finding her and bringing her home."

"How will you do that?"

"Have you heard from Julianne Eaton?"

"Not yet. Is that your plan? To shift the attention to sex offenders?"

"If need be, yes. But that's not why I called. I need you to meet with Wren Priestly."

"When?"

"Now."

"Right now?"

"As soon as you can get back downtown. She saw the press conference, and she's threatening to pull the funds for the tip line and reward."

I slapped my hand against the basin. "She can't do that!"

"Yes, Kris, she can."

"I can't leave Gwen and Tracey alone. They're falling apart."

"More than before?"

"Much. Tracey's upstairs sobbing, and Gwen's standing by the front door, waiting for the police to start searching the house."

"I'll send a lawyer. One of the women on our board is a criminal defense attorney. I'll ask if she can represent them or recommend someone."

"They don't want a lawyer."

"Whether or not they think they need one, they do. Tell them not to say anything until I can get someone there. Are the protestors still outside?"

"Yes."

"What about the Pride Riders?"

"About six or eight of them are standing around on the lawn."

"Could you ask one of them to come inside the house?"

"I don't think Gwen and Tracey would be comfortable with that."

"Well, I can't get away right now. I'm in the middle of coordinating everything for the neighborhood meeting. I have piles of phone messages sitting on my desk. Where's Fran? Why isn't she there?"

"I'm not sure," I said, narrowly avoiding a direct lie. The last thing I wanted to tell Destiny was that Fran was busy digging up dirt on Tracey. "I'll call her."

"Even if you can't get reach Fran, you need to leave now. Wren lives in that new building across from the Denver Art Museum. I told her you'd be there within the hour."

I cracked open the bathroom door and glanced worriedly at Gwen, who hadn't budged from where I'd left her. "Couldn't I stay for a few more minutes, just until—"

"If we lose this money," Destiny said in a clipped tone, "we lose the best chance we have of finding Kayla alive."

My call to Fran went straight to voice mail.

In a hushed tone, I left an urgent message for her, then exited the bathroom and explained to Gwen that I had to leave to meet with a supporter about the tip line and reward—not bothering to elaborate that my contact was our sole contributor on the verge of reneging.

On the way to my car, I asked one of the Pride Riders to keep an eye on the two women inside the house, and I glanced at the cops, who seemed in no rush to make their next move.

The drive from Highlands Ranch to 13th and Broadway took about forty-five minutes, putting me on the plaza outside the Museum Residences at one o'clock.

Across from the Denver Art Museum and steps from the state capitol and Colorado History Museum, the five-story, fifty-five unit condominium project stood as the most expensive real estate, per square foot, in Denver. Designed by Daniel Libeskind, the building was fabricated out of glass and steel and complemented the Hamilton Building, an art museum addition also drawn up by the world-renowned architect.

When Wren Priestly opened the door to her top floor unit, and I stepped onto the black oak flooring, the three walls of glass, none of which were straight, made me feel like I was standing on air. From the middle of the living room, I could see the titanium hull of the museum jutting across 13th Avenue, the bluish range of the Rocky Mountains in the distance and the gold dome of the capitol to the east.

Black and taupe furnishings did little to break the monochromatic look of the space, and the triangular windows, high concrete ceilings and explosion of reds and oranges in the abstract art threw me off-kilter, a sensation my ultra-rich hostess did nothing to ease.

Within minutes of my arrival, she'd served expensive bottled water that made me burp and casually mentioned her second, third and fourth homes in Idaho Springs, Napa Valley and Cape Cod. She'd dropped the name of practically every famous lesbian who lived in Los Angeles and seated us at a dining room table made from 42,000-year-old wood.

The world's oldest workable timber had come from an island off New Zealand, where a Kauri tree had remained buried for tens of thousands of years without rotting or petrifying before coming to rest in Wren Priestly's home. In the shape of a half-circle, the table had distinctive grain patterns and hues of gold and cognac, but it wouldn't have merited a second glance if Wren hadn't extolled its ancient and sacred properties. I was afraid to put my elbows on it, much less a drink, so I balanced the bottle of water in my lap, awkwardly holding on to its deep-blue neck as Wren continued her monologue.

"I'm a change agent. I built a global company before I turned forty and achieved the Forbes Four Hundred list two years later. I spent the first half of my life making money, and I'm spending the last half giving it away."

"That's admirable," I said half-heartedly.

"Some people view money as power. I view it as a tool for social change. I seeded the United Lesbian Foundation the year Amendment Two passed," Wren said, referring to a Colorado ballot issue that had been written to repeal anti-discrimination laws for gays and lesbians. "The foundation now has an endowment of thirty million, and, of course, I prevented the amendment from becoming law. Last year,

I spent five hundred thousand dollars turning both houses of the state Legislature over to the Democrats. Over the past ten years, I've contributed millions toward candidates who run against politicians known for anti-gay stances. I have a significant investment in this community."

"Obviously."

"I can unequivocally control the success *or failure* of anything I choose."

"Okay," I said in a wary tone.

"Yesterday morning, I gave fifty thousand dollars to what I thought was a worthwhile cause."

"It still is."

"Assure me, please, that my contribution won't be disbursed to some drug-addicted informant who turns in Gwen Martin and Tracey Reid for a crime they committed weeks ago."

"I can't control that." I looked at Wren intently. "Where are you getting your information?"

"From women in the community who share my concern that my name's attached to this cause."

"Your donation was anonymous."

"Yes, but naturally people assume I'm the benefactor. Tell me I didn't make a big mistake when I called Destiny Greaves to offer my support."

"You didn't."

"What do you know about Gwen and Tracey? Can they be trusted to represent us?"

"I don't think they hurt Kayla."

"That's not my point. Enlighten me about their characters."

"What enlightenment do you need? I just came from Highlands Ranch, where two women are trying to deal with the worst thing that's ever happened to them. Somehow, they're managing to do it with grace and dignity."

"How they're handling themselves at present is only half the equation. Tell me about their backgrounds."

I met her stare. "I can't."

"Can't or won't?"

"Both. Number one, I don't know that much. Number two, Gwen and Tracey deserve the right to privacy."

"Not if my credibility's at stake. What—" Wren broke off, her brow furrowed.

I pulled my phone out of my pocket, silenced the ringer and glanced at the screen. "If you'll excuse me for a minute, I need to take this call."

"By all means," Wren said, her tone implying less tolerance. She rose and stood by the window, in what appeared to be a measured pose. The tan fedora, cashmere turtleneck, red velvet jacket with buttons as large as silver dollars and black riding pants—it was a look. One that was accentuated by her acrylic nails, jet black hair and mist tan.

"Hello."

"Hey, boss," Fran said excitedly. "Never believe what—"

I interrupted. "I'm in the middle of a meeting."

"With the gals?"

"No."

After a long pause, Fran said, "Can't talk?"

"That sounds right."

"Fallout from the Keystone Cop press conference?"

"Probably. If you could go by the house and take a look, I'd really appreciate it."

"Pine Lane abode?"

"That's the one."

"Need me to babysit the mothers?"

"Urgently."

"On my way. You coming, too?"

"As soon as I can."

"Ten-four."

"Thanks for getting back with me so promptly. You're done with your other call?"

"Wrapped up the Shelby Valentine interview a few minutes ago. Man, oh man, Tracey's ex-squeeze had a whopper of a tale to tell. Got a master criminal on our hands."

"Not—" I said, breaking off. I couldn't complete the sentence. I just couldn't.

"Yep. None other. Mother Tracey. Ring me when you can."

"Thanks. I will," I said, closing the phone.

CHAPTER 13

I put my arms on the table and could barely stop myself from cradling my head in my hands.

"My decision to continue to participate in this project or *not* participate shouldn't be taken lightly," Wren said, returning to her seat.

"I'm sorry about that. I have a sewer pipe backing up, and I'd left a message for the plumber. You know how they are."

"All I know is that my foundation might be associated with something unpleasant, and I'd prefer you focus on that."

I put the phone back in my pocket. "What did you hope to accomplish by donating the reward money?"

"To bring Kayla—"

"Wren, please," I cut in. "Bottom line. What did you really want?"

She released a faint smile. "To bring attention to the Martin-Reid family. To seed change. I won the battle for gay couples to adopt children in the state of Colorado. That became legal last month. Next, I want gay marriage."

"How does Kayla's disappearance relate?"

"Whatever task I undertake, I employ a simple management philosophy. Understand what needs to be achieved. Determine who can contribute. Put actions in motion to reach that goal."

"I don't understand."

"When I heard about Kayla Martin, it fit with my objectives. For every dollar I spend, I expect three in return value."

I raised an eyebrow. "So you expected your fifty thousand in reward money would buy a hundred and fifty thousand dollars worth of publicity and goodwill toward lesbians?"

"To be blunt, yes."

"If that was your only objective, you might have chosen the wrong couple."

Wren looked me in the eye, unblinking. "I became acutely aware of that at one minute past noon today. Six minutes later, I called Destiny Greaves to schedule a time to strategize where we go from here. I'm disappointed she couldn't make it a priority to meet with me personally. Apparently, the reward and tip line aren't her highest priorities."

"Destiny's taking action steps that could lead to finding Kayla," I said, careful to keep my tone even. "She's preparing for a press conference this afternoon to rebut the police chief's stance. She's also organizing a meeting for six o'clock in Highlands Ranch, the focus of which will be the threat registered sex offenders pose to the community. Otherwise, she'd be here."

"Good for her, but my immediate concern is how to limit my exposure in the event the situation worsens."

"You don't care whether Kayla lives or dies?"

"Assuming the child isn't dead already, yes. I would prefer she lives, but that's almost beside the point. It was never my motivation for offering the reward."

"You wanted to draw attention to the plight of lesbian

mothers?"

"Precisely. I view my involvement as a means to an end."

"Because Kayla's mothers haven't lived up to the standards you've set for them as role models, you'd rather not have your name associated with this cause?"

"Is that unreasonable?"

"Yes. Because at this exact moment, someone might be doing whatever he pleases to a three-year-old girl. Or, Kayla's already been murdered, and the killer is walking free."

Wren shrugged. "Revamping the justice system doesn't align with my goals."

"Your goal is the positive portrayal of lesbians?"

She smiled tightly. "We understand each other."

"And the only way we'll ever pass muster—in the media or in society—is to act perfectly. To live our lives without fault?"

"Societal change happens in waves. That's been proven through thousands of years of documented history."

"In your scheme, the good lesbians will infiltrate first, eventually paving the way for the bad lesbians?"

"Your phrasing is coarse, but that's the general idea."

I cocked my head and studied her. "How will we know the good ones from the bad?"

"Don't be obtuse."

"No, really," I said, my voice splitting with anger. "Tell me. Who's going to be in your so-called first wave, and who will always have to hide, no matter how many waves crash through?"

"This rhetoric isn't productive. Let's turn to a topic that might interest you personally."

"Such as?"

"If I'm not mistaken, the money I award the Lesbian Community Center every year represents a significant portion of the operating budget. A budget which, in turn, funds Destiny Greaves's salary."

I didn't move a face muscle. "What's your point?"

"Fix this, or your partner will lose her job and the Center," Wren said, her eyes flashing.

• • •

"What an arrogant bitch," I screamed to Fran as soon as I was back in my car.

"Wrench?"

"I had to hear about how she was fluent in three languages by the time she was thirteen."

"BFD. Reverse would be more impressive. Thirteen tongues by three. Enough about her, though. Gotta cool off your hot head and get back in the game. We got bigger problems than that little bird."

"You're at the house with Gwen and Tracey?"

"Yep, along with everyone else. It's a circus down here. Three-ringer."

"What's going on?"

"News copters hovering. Photographers and reporters lined up and down the cul-de-sac. Officers carting out bags and boxes of materials."

"What have they taken?"

"Name it. Tore apart Kayla's room. Took the bedding and rug. Hauled off Tracey's computers. Taking snapshots of everything."

"Did they see the broken television?"

"Right off the bat. Bagged up bits and pieces of it."

"Damn it!"

"Team in the backyard's searching with radar."

"For a body?"

"Bingo. Fascinating stuff," Fran said, sounding short of breath. "Divided the area into a grid using orange flags. Maybe fifty, sixty squares in all. Now taking this gizmo—looks like a disk on a pole— and running it back and forth over the lawn and garden, around the brick path and lilacs. Special ground-penetrating radar detects disturbances in the soil. Electromagnetic waves go down, four feet to a hundred feet, depending on the dirt and rocks. Clear signal, good news. Static, not so good. They plunk down red flags, mark the spot for further investigation."

"How many suspicious areas have they flagged?"

"Ten or twelve, most near the jungle gym."

"Jesus!"

"No worries. Six coppers are standing by with shovels, but no one's turned a scoop of dirt."

"What are Gwen and Tracey doing?"

"Gwen's in the living room confabbing with the lawyer Destiny sent. Cute gal, but a little on the thin side. Tracey's sitting in her office staring out the window into the backyard."

"Where are you?"

"Right below her. Dining room. Front-row view of the backyard search. What the heck?" Fran exclaimed.

"Fran!" I said, after a long gap.

"Sorry. Gotta go. Cadaver dog's nosing under the rose bush."

Before I could toss the phone onto the passenger seat, it rang again.

"What happened with Wren?" Destiny said by way of greeting.

"She's leaving the reward in place."

"Thank God!"

"But she could pull it at any moment. If this blows up, she'll crucify you. She made that very clear."

"I expected as much."

"You'll be looking for a new career."

"Wren Priestly threatened me?"

"More or less. She doesn't have that much influence, does she?"

"Probably," Destiny said in a resigned tone.

"How?"

"She'd pull her own funds, then she'd have a quiet word with all of the major donors to the Center—philanthropists, foundations, agencies. Her name attached to a project brings instant credibility. Likewise, her withdrawal from something . . ." Destiny's voice trailed off.

"What about your individual contributors? Wren can't sway all of them."

"Their donations make up about ten percent of our annual budget."

"Shit."

"How do you feel about me coming to work for you and Fran?"

"Are you serious?"

Destiny laughed nervously. "The way things are going, I might not have a choice. The phone's been ringing off the hook since the police press conference. Women are backing away from their offers of support. We might have to cancel the search I was organizing for Saturday."

"Don't do that yet. Today's only Tuesday."

"An activist from Ohio, Lara Jaworski, called to tell me that I'm making the biggest mistake of my career. She told me it was my job to look at the big picture and act in the best interests of the greater good."

"In a convoluted way, I think that was Wren's contention."

"Lara took the time out of her busy day," Destiny said tersely, "to remind me that just because someone identifies as LGBT doesn't automatically make her a good mother. Our community has the same problems as every other community and the same potential for evil acts. As if I'm living in a hallucinatory state and don't know that! But am I supposed to support every lesbian, or only the ones who conform to my idea of acceptable?"

Before I could answer, Destiny continued heatedly. "Down the line, Lara assured me, I'll regret taking this stand if I lose the support of the police and go up against other community leaders. Three years ago, she supported a Toledo couple accused of child abuse, and when they were arrested and convicted, it backfired on her and the local center. The mothers received a thirty-year prison sentence, Lara resigned because of health problems caused by stress, and the community was never the same again. Why would she call to tell me this shit? How does she think her so-called sharing brings me any closer to finding Kayla Martin?"

"Maybe she has a point."

"I'm in the middle of writing notes for my press conference.

What's your point?"

"You're giving the press conference?"

"Yes. I told you earlier."

"I thought you were coordinating it, not giving it. Why can't Gwen or Tracey speak to the press?"

"Because Tracey's lost her voice, and Gwen's on the verge of a nervous breakdown. Isn't that what you told me two hours ago?" There was a long silence before Destiny spoke again, this time more calmly. "You don't think one of them had anything to do with this, do you, Kris? Tell me the truth."

"I know what you want to hear, but I can't give you that answer."

"You believe they hurt her?"

I let out a long exhale. "I don't know. I honestly don't. They both seem like good parents, but you never know what people do behind closed doors. Or what they're capable of doing in a split second of anger. Maybe one of them struck her and accidentally killed her."

"Then what? Where's the body? Did they throw her away like a piece of garbage? Can you hear yourself? None of this makes sense."

"Neither does the fact that a three-year-old wandered off in the middle of the day, never to be seen again. Or that at the exact moment Tracey was in a deep sleep, a stranger walked in the back door, crept up the stairs and snatched Kayla from her bed. They live in suburbia, Destiny. There's no way to sit on that cul-de-sac for hours on end, stalking a victim. Not without being noticed. There are no cars on the street—day or night. All the residents park in their garages. There's no foot traffic. How could Kayla's abduction have been random?"

"Stop." Destiny sounded on the verge of tears. "This doesn't help. What would you suggest I do?"

"Not be so publicly involved."

"It's a little late for that."

"Let Fran and I do some checking behind the scenes. Find out more about Gwen and Tracey."

"No!"

"Why not?"

"It's a betrayal. If they ever found out—"

"They wouldn't."

"No, Kris. You can't do that to them."

"I wouldn't be doing it *to* them. I would be doing it *for* you. To save you from—"

"I don't need saving. Kayla Martin needs saving. Every minute you spend looking into the potential guilt of her mothers is one less you give her. Promise me you won't—" Destiny said before breaking off abruptly. "I'm sorry. I have to go. That's a Denver officer on the other line, returning my call."

My stomach churned. "Why did you call the Denver police?"

"To report death threats. Three today alone."

"Against Gwen and Tracey?"

"Against me."

CHAPTER 14

Someone wanted to kill Destiny.

That wasn't all that unusual. Over the course of her career as an activist, she'd received hundreds of death threats, but three in one day?

On the drive to Highlands Ranch, I had forty-five minutes to obsess about how I'd live without her if one of the lunatics followed through. By the time I arrived at Pine Lane, my head was spinning, and my emotions were reeling between rage and despair.

Because of congestion near the Martin-Reid house, I parked two blocks away. Walking toward the hubbub, I saw a police tow truck driving away with Gwen's Nissan Altima on the flatbed.

Fran was squatting in the driveway, taking stock of the spectacle, which by now included protestors, supporters, news crews, neighbors and law enforcement personnel. In a denim floppy hat and orange

T-shirt with purple lettering, *Keep Your Prayers To Yourself*, Fran stood out from the rest of the crowd.

"Piece of good news," she whispered loudly when I was within earshot. "Had a chat with one of the geologists. Tall guy in charge of the sonar search. About to rule out the property as a crime scene. Backyard anyway."

"Thank God!" I moved into the shade of the Highlands Ranch Police Department crime lab truck. "Where's Tracey's Explorer?"

"Fuzz carted that off first. Calm down," she said, apparently in response to my violent head movements. "Got the situation under control. Already sent two of the Pride Riders to Hertz with the Platinum card. Hope you don't mind. Made an executive decision without you."

"Not at all."

"Charge the car rental to the business. Least we can do. Prides should be back in an hour or so with a car the gals can share. Gwen, especially, needs wheels. Those searches she does every day, only thing keeping her from cracking up."

"You made the right call." I stepped closer to her and lowered my voice. "What happened with Shelby Valentine?"

Fran glanced around furtively. "Not here. Meet me inside, and I'll fill you in on the ex."

"Where?"

"Master bath." Her eyes darted back and forth. "Confab in five. Take separate routes."

I walked through the front door of the house, nodded at Gwen, who was on the couch, deep in discussion with a woman in a peach pantsuit, and headed up the stairs.

As I passed Tracey in her office, she tore her attention away from the window and called out, "Kris, can I talk to you?" She'd changed out of her pajamas and into a black skirt, flip-flops and a gray zip-up sweatshirt. The hoodie was pulled tight, covering her hair, leaving only the pale oval of her face exposed.

"In a second. I have to use the restroom."

She nodded almost imperceptibly, and I hurried off. I cut through the master bedroom and into the bathroom, where Fran was perched on the edge of the jetted tub.

She peered through the slats of the blinds. "Strange girl."

"Tracey?"

"Sierra Frazier. Spends too much time in those kung fu poses."

I leaned over the tub, my head inches from Fran's. "Tae Kwon Do. She has a brown belt."

"Something's off kilter."

"How so?" I transferred my gaze from the Frazier backyard to the one below me. Through the ivy on the cedar pergola, I saw six policemen chatting on the flagstone patio. The tranquility of the setting—complete with lush Kentucky bluegrass, stands of aspen, bird feeders and a brick walkway with moss growing through it—was marred by dozens of yellow and red flags.

"Squirt came over earlier to add a toy to the shrine. Tenth toy or stuffed animal she's brought. Wonder if she nicked them from Kayla in the first place. Probably bringing 'em back out of guilt."

"Maybe she's interested in what's going on. I never saw anything like this when I was nine years old. Or any other age."

"True enough. Viewing everything in a new light myself today. Halogen, not candle."

"In regards to Sierra?"

"Tracey. Shelby Valentine had a tale to tell." Fran pulled a small spiral notebook from her pocket, flipped it open and held it at arm's length. "Give it to you in chronological order. Two met six years ago, at the Painted Rose, on Shelby's fiftieth birthday. Gift that kept on taking."

"What?"

"Little inside joke." Fran chuckled. "Where was I?"

I leaned against the double-sink vanity. "The Painted Rose."

"Lesbian bar on Tejon Street. Fell in love during two-step and cowboy cha-cha. Dances," Fran said, in response to my puzzled look. "Moved in together the first night they shared the sheets, which happened to be the second date. Tracey wormed her way into Shelby's artist pad in northwest Denver. Saw it this morning. Quite the fun house, and don't mean that as a compliment. Bathroom decked out in shells and jewels. Mosaics everywhere. Christmas tree still up in the corner of the living room—fully loaded. Hanging beads for doors, chandelier made out of wine glasses. Orange walls, purple ceilings, blue furniture. Yikes!"

"Could you speed it up? A minute ago, Tracey asked to talk to me, and I'm supposed to be using the bathroom."

"Might have to pretend you're plugged up." Fran shrugged. "Just saying, place was distracting. Could barely concentrate on my note taking. Didn't help that Shelby's ditzy. Scattered, but not bad looking. Needs some sun. Complexion like a corpse. Stringy, shoulder-length hair doesn't help. Looked wet. Why do women use that much gel?"

"Fran!"

"Wore a black men's blazer and blue jeans. Not too fond of the look myself, but—" she said before reacting to my glare and adding hastily, "back to the past. Everything was hunky-dory between Shelby and Tracey, year one. Shelby was doing her murals, painting them inside restaurants and bars. Tracey was trotting off to her job, assistant to a real estate developer. No worries until month thirteen when Shell-shocked took the fatal trip to Target."

"Fatal?"

Fran grinned. "Slight exaggeration. More like fateful. Went to pay for a buggy's worth of items, credit card was declined. Opened her billfold. No cash. No cards. Hightailed it home. Lo and behold, no money in her online banking account. No Trace."

"Shit."

Fran nodded solemnly. "Double-deuce crap. By day's end, Shelby found out the house was in foreclosure, she had thirty-seven grand in credit card debt, and all her Schwabbies had been emptied."

"Stock accounts?"

"Yes, ma'am. Shellacked searched the house, top to bottom. Found a desk full of demand-for-payment letters and thirty cents in a change jar they kept on the kitchen counter. Sum total of what was left."

"Tracey had stolen from her?"

"Every cent she had. Some she didn't. Amount taken, plus amount borrowed, total came to six-figures. Almost sent the woman to BK land."

"Fran," I said, a warning in my tone.

"Sorry. Personal bankruptcy."

"How did Tracey pull it off?"

"Ingenuity and forgery. Added her own name to the deed on the house by signing Shelby's Jane Hancock. Started borrowing against it. Bills got sent to a post office box. Opened credit cards in Shelby's name using her social and date of birth. Again with the P.O. Box. Took cash advances off the cards. Knew Shelby's favorite passwords and PINs—who doesn't use the same ones all the time? Used inside info to empty the bank and stock accounts. Simple deal, really."

"Why didn't Shelby discover any of this as it was happening?"

"Woman's no bean counter. Numbers bore her. Turned over the bill-paying chores to Tracey early on in the love affair. Never opened the mail. Never listened to voice mail messages on the home phone. Thought the T-woman was taking care of all that. Little did she know, creditors'd been on her heels for months, nipping away."

"What an idiot!"

"Artsy type. Overly trusting, but not an idiot. Think misguided fool in love. Why you looking so angry?"

"This is going to ruin Destiny. She's gone out on a limb for these two women," I hissed.

"Limb breaks, she'll still land on her feet."

"If this controversy damages Wren Priestly, she'll bury Destiny. She'll never work as an activist again. Wren told me that point-blank."

"You pass on the bird's threat to Destiny?"

"Yes, and it didn't phase her. Destiny's doing what she thinks is right, and if it doesn't work out, she kids that she'll come work with us."

Fran frowned. "*With?*"

"For us. Whatever."

"Can't have that happening."

"Tell me about it." I sighed. "How many people know about Tracey's theft? Did Shelby press charges?"

"Not a one. Shelby talked to a district attorney who told her fraud's about impossible to prove when the two parties co-habitate. Also, has a few skeletons of her own to hide."

"Shelby? What are they?"

Fran wrinkled her nose. "Doesn't necessarily declare all her income to all the necessary agencies."

"What are you talking about?"

"Takes in money off the books. Was afraid if she launched a grenade at Tracey, woman might send back a missile. Bottom line, our friend Tracey got a pass on three Colorado Criminal Code biggies. Theft by deception, theft by check and theft by misrepresentation."

"Where did the stolen money go?"

Fran raised an eyebrow. "That's the hundred-thousand-dollar question. Shelby hired a private eye to trace the assets. Fellow by the name of Donald Washburn. Big rummy. Met him at last month's association meeting. Man couldn't find money, in a bank, if he was standing in the vault. If it weren't a conflict of interest, would have given Shelby Valentine a few tips myself. Remember that course I took in July on hiding assets and disappearing?"

"Mmm," I said vaguely.

"At the Holiday Inn. Ate a moldy muffin and felt puny all day."

"Ah."

"Any-hoo, between trips to the bathroom, learned a few tricks of the trade. Without-A-Trace could have purchased traveler's checks or cashier's checks. Could have bought gold coins or bullions. And, of course, the tried and true. Could have stashed Ben Franklins under the mattress."

"Or she could have spent it all on meth."

"True enough. In any case, Shelby'll never see a dime of that money."

"Did Shelby know about Tracey's addiction?"

"Said she didn't."

"How did Shelby save her house?"

"Eighty-year-old mum cashed in her life savings to help with the refinance. But enough about the mark. Concentrate on the con for a minute. Primary requirement to pull off a convoluted heist? Nerves of steel. Picture our friend T.R. getting into bed every night with her prey, then climbing into her pockets every day."

I groaned. "You know what this means?"

"Indeed, I do."

"Tracey Reid's a liar."

Fran sucked her teeth. "World class."

CHAPTER 15

"I was raised by liars," Tracey said, the first words she spoke when I joined her in the office. She looked gaunt and weary, and her mouth was set in a grim line. "They made me feel like everything I did was wrong. The only time I felt right was when I was high."

I sat on the chair next to her and consciously avoided looking at the bare spots where her computer equipment had rested. "Your parents were liars?"

"I don't remember them. My mother got rid of me when I was ten months old. I'm referring to my money-hungry foster parents, my failed adoptive parents, my cover-your-ass counselors at group homes, practically every adult I met. They all lied, and meth was my only truth. It got rid of the feelings I never wanted to feel. It gave me such a rush. All I wanted to do was experience that again."

"The rush?"

"The confidence. With meth, I was in charge. It helped me feel like I belonged. I still fantasize about it sometimes," she said, staring at me fixedly. "I think about the crystal going into the pipe, changing from solid to liquid to gas. The inhale and the euphoria. The all-night highs. The week-long binges. Meth was my best friend. Meth erased everything bad."

"That must have been appealing."

Tracey smiled ruefully. "Until it made everything worse."

"When did you start using?"

"On my nineteenth birthday. I'd done just about everything else before then—alcohol, pot, pain meds, coke."

"Did you become addicted right away?"

"More or less." She paused before adding, "Yes."

"When did you stop?"

"Three years later. My maternal grandparents paid for me to go into rehab. I went along with their plan, but I was still acting the first week I was at the center. When I met Gwen, though, everything changed. She was my reason for quitting, something to stay clean for."

"She was there getting treatment?"

Tracey nodded. "She came in a week after me, and we fell in love instantly, the first time we saw each other across a room. When we were still in treatment, we made a pact that we'd never use meth again. We swore to each other that if one of us did, even once, we'd break up. No second chances. If we went back to any old friends or hangouts or destructive patterns, we would lose the relationship. The threat was our motivation for getting and staying clean. We had to choose something that had a stronger hold than the drug. We chose each other."

"It must have worked."

She sighed deeply. "We've had five miraculous years together. I miss her."

"Kayla?"

"Gwen. She believes Kayla's coming home. Any minute. She feels it in her heart, but I know my daughter's gone. I'm as certain of that as I've ever been of anything in my life, but I can't talk to Gwen. She won't listen. I've lost her, too."

I reached over to touch Tracey's knee. "Not for good. This is a wretched time. No one could cope with what you two have been through, but you'll be close again."

"We've never slept apart. Not one night since we left rehab, not unless Gwen was out of town. Now, she won't let me near her."

"She will again. I'm sure—"

"Thursday, I thought I was in the worst nightmare anyone could imagine, but it keeps getting worse." Tracey pointed toward the empty desk and the window. "Why are they searching our house and yard?"

"The police are trained to suspect the people closest to the victim. I know it doesn't seem like it, but that might be a good thing. With this much scrutiny and processing, they can eliminate you and Gwen as potential suspects."

"Why us? Why aren't they going after Bruce?"

"He's never showed that much of an interest in Kayla, has he?"

"Not until we cut off his visits in February. Our original agreement called for a favor, not a father. We asked for a two-minute commitment on his part. From the beginning, I told Gwen we shouldn't allow Bruce in Kayla's life, but that would have meant Gwen had to stop being friends with him. She wouldn't listen to me. I can't win," Tracey said, running her hands across the hoodie. "I got clean. I turned my life around, and now everything I've done, said or been is being questioned."

"I hate to add to that that scrutiny," I said gingerly, "but Destiny told me that the Highlands Ranch police have uncovered a juvenile arrest on your record."

She rolled her eyes and shook her head aggressively. "For assault. When I was sixteen and living in my sixth residential facility, I slapped a girl in the face, and she fell to the floor. That was my big teen crime."

"They're also connecting you to an ID theft ring."

She laughed, a desperate sound. "Because my name gets misspelled all the time?"

"They've found items in a storage locker."

"Oh," she said in a small voice.

"You know about this?"

She looked frightened. "Years ago, I shared a storage locker with one of my meth friends, Marla. I'd forgotten all about it. When I came out of rehab, I took out my stuff. I haven't paid rent or been to the storage facility in years. The police think something in the locker belongs to me?"

"Evidently."

"Oh, God!" Tracey said, sounding panicked. "What did they find?"

"A scanner. Software for printing payroll checks. Fake IDs."

She swallowed hard. "It must be Marla's."

"You and Marla didn't steal money from people?"

She met my gaze and said only after a long silence, "I took money from someone I lived with. I never ripped off anyone else."

"Have you told the attorney downstairs?"

"Lillian? No. She told me and Gwen that we each need our own attorney, and she's representing Gwen. She called one of her friends from law school, who's supposed to come over and talk to me." Tracey covered her mouth with both hands. "No one will believe me, will they?"

"When the lawyer gets here, you need to level with her. Tell her everything."

She blinked rapidly as she nodded. "All I kept asking every family who took me in was, 'Please, no more homes.' But I'd be sent to another one, over and over again, until I lost count. I would never do that to my daughter. I made sacrifices every day to ensure that Kayla had the perfect life. I agreed to move here. I stayed home with her. I joined play groups. I did everything in my power to fit in so that Kayla could have a normal childhood. You have to believe me. Please, Kris, do you believe me?"

"Tracey, I'm not the one—" I stammered.

"I haven't lied since I came out of rehab. Not once. Not to myself or anyone else. Never to Gwen—" she broke off.

"Until?"

Tracey wouldn't look at me. "Last Thursday."

Before I could respond, we both jumped at the sound of banging on the door.

"Sorry to interrupt," Fran said, barging in. "Julianne Eaton's trying to track you down, Kris. Sent an e-mail with the info you need. Wants to know if you have any questions."

I shot Fran a look. "Could you tell her that I'll call her back?"

Fran cast a quick glance at Tracey, who was bent over, her head touching her chest. "Will do. Anything else?"

"No," I muttered, and Fran took the hint and backed out of the room, but it was too late.

Despite my gentle prodding, almost begging, Tracey refused to elaborate on her lie, the one she'd told on the day her daughter disappeared.

CHAPTER 16

With every failed attempt, my frustration mounted.

So much for a $2,000 laptop, $200 portable printer and $69 per month in broadband charges.

When I urgently needed the technology to perform, it failed.

After I'd left Tracey, I'd rushed to my car only to find that I couldn't open the attachment from Julianne Eaton. Rather than continue to fiddle with the equipment from inside my car, I decided to return to the office, where I had Julianne fax me a copy of the sex offender profiles she'd finally obtained from her FBI friend.

Thirty minutes later, I felt like barfing.

Ken Bosworth and Todd Robie.

These were the two convicted sex offenders Freddie Sampson, the FBI agent, had determined were the most likely to have abducted Kayla. In her report, Freddie had included photographs of the men and personal fact sheets, which I studied with equal degrees of care and disgust.

Suspect number one, Ken Bosworth, was a sixty-two-year-old man with ruddy cheeks, bug eyes and a bald crown. By his innocuous, bespectacled looks, he could have been a minister or an accountant. In fact, he was a convicted sex offender with twenty years' experience. Among other charges, he'd been found guilty of sex offense against a child, indecent assault against a child, lewd conduct involving a child and fondling a child. His victims had included girls and boys, ages four to fifteen, and he'd served full sentences in Florida. That meant he wasn't bound by parole, supervision or counseling. He'd moved in with his sister eighteen months earlier, and his current address was listed as 8632 South Red Quill Drive, three blocks from Kayla's home. He loosely fit the description of the man Tracey and Kayla had noticed in the park.

Suspect number two, Todd Robie, was thirty-five years old, with scraggly brown hair, a patchy beard and slits for eyes. He, too, was living in the Meadowridge subdivision, at 8733 South Ridgeback Circle. He'd earned his sentence by molesting an unaccompanied four-year-old girl when he worked at a Fort Collins department store. After serving four years in prison, he'd been released ten days earlier. Five days before Kayla went missing.

Two prime suspects.

Had either man appeared on the Highlands Ranch Police Department's list of "persons of interest," or were the detectives in charge of Kayla's case so intent on pursuing Gwen and Tracey that they'd let two known criminals escape their notice?

I was afraid I knew the answer.

Unfortunately, I didn't have a clue what to do about it.

At four o'clock, I turned on the television at the office, just in time to catch the opening remarks of Destiny's live press conference.

"The odds weren't good to begin with, and Gwen Martin and Tracey Reid are aware that they worsen with each passing hour. Still, they're desperately searching for their three-year-old daughter."

Truthfully, not they. Gwen, I thought.

"The Highlands Ranch Police Department might have stopped looking for Kayla Martin, but Gwen and Tracey haven't. Every day, they hope this will be the day their daughter comes home. The police have implied that Kayla's mothers have been less than cooperative, but this simply isn't true."

Across Destiny's chest, at the bottom of the screen, a banner scrolled, crediting her as the "Martin family spokeswoman" and "Executive Director of the Lesbian Community Center."

"They've had their property searched, they've given DNA samples and they've submitted to multiple interrogations. It's only in recent hours, when the direction of the investigation seems to have drastically changed course, that, on the advice of their lawyer, they've refused to be interrogated further."

Technically, lawyers. Plural.

Destiny paused and looked directly into the camera. "If the police have adequate evidence, why aren't they bringing charges? Gwen Martin and Tracey Reid should be presumed innocent—by the police, the media and the citizens of this community—until proven otherwise. They are a committed, loving couple who has been targeted unfairly because of their sexuality, and, clearly, the investigation is now biased. An atmosphere of presumed guilt surrounds this case, when others, who aren't lesbians, would have been afforded the presumption of innocence."

Well stated!

"Over the years, like any two human beings, Gwen and Tracey have had their share of challenges, but who among us could stand up under the scrutiny to which these two women have been subjected in the past five days? A large part of the focus has been on which of them is the, quote, 'true' mother, and the question alone diminishes the role and importance they both share as caregivers. The options of domestic partnership or lesbian marriage are, unfortunately, not available to Gwen and Tracey in the state of Colorado. If they were, they would have taken advantage of those legal ties and benefits long ago. Instead, Gwen and Tracey have made the strongest pledge they can to each other—to be life partners and equal parents."

Too political. Get back on track, Destiny.

"At this, the worst time in their lives, they've been subjected to innuendo, false accusations and death threats because of their sexuality. They're living under siege, with news helicopters flying over their home, television satellite trucks taking over their street, and anti-gay protestors swarming their sidewalk. People say this case isn't being handled any differently, but it is. For example, the Loralei Recovery Foundation had promised to send a hundred volunteers from Texas to Highlands Ranch this coming Saturday, to aid in the search for Kayla. Yesterday, the Foundation broke that promise for no reason other than that Kayla Martin's parents are lesbians. The organization backed out of its pledge to Kayla and to our community, and every time prejudice goes unchallenged, it fosters more prejudice. As another example of discrimination, for the past two days, groups from Sacred Life Church in southeast Denver have been screaming foul language at Gwen and Tracey from the sidewalk in front of their home."

Foul language. Score another one for Destiny. To my knowledge, no Bible-beater had uttered a cuss word, but their language did indeed qualify as foul.

"Fortunately, Gwen and Tracey have received tremendous support from within the lesbian community. On Sunday, more than two hundred volunteers assembled at Founders Park in Highlands Ranch and searched nine square miles. We were out from dawn until dusk, working all day, stopping only for brief, mandated breaks. At the time, we were optimistic about the results of the search. We found things we were told could help the Highlands Ranch Police Department determine the whereabouts of Kayla. Whether that evidence has been processed, in light of the direction the investigation seems to be taking, is a valid question."

Brilliant. Show the community's belief in the mothers. Put the burden on the police.

"I've asked Gwen and Tracey directly if they had any involvement in Kayla's disappearance, and they've both answered no. Emphatically. Yet, it's obvious the police are narrowing their focus at a time when it should be expanding. We've learned from a source inside law enforcement that there are thirty-four registered sex offenders residing in Highlands Ranch, any one of whom could have abducted Kayla Martin."

Source inside law enforcement. Freddie Sampson from the FBI. A masterful slant.

"We're asking for the public's help in locating Kayla Martin." Destiny held up a photo of Kayla. "We need to bring her home safely. If you have any information at all, something you might not have known was relevant at the time, please call the tip line or nine-one-one."

Nice touch. Tip line first. Authorities second.

"An anonymous lesbian donor has been kind enough to contribute fifty thousand dollars as a reward for information leading to the arrest and conviction of whoever took Kayla Martin from her home on Thursday, September thirteenth."

Smooth move. Back Wren Priestly into a corner. Don't allow her to break her word.

"Someone knows something. A little girl can't just vanish into thin air. As a final note, I'd ask that from this point forward, you respect the privacy of Gwen and Tracey. They need to put all of their energies toward finding their daughter. Thank you."

Classy, touching conclusion.

"Two's company. Three's a crowd."

"Huh?" I replied absentmindedly to Fran. I was preoccupied, surveying the crowd of anxious suburbanites.

We'd taken the last two seats in the last row at the Meadowridge clubhouse and were surrounded by women in Capri pants and tight blouses and men in khaki pants and golf shirts. Forty chairs were occupied, and another thirty or forty residents had crammed into the sides and back of the room.

"Destiny. Working for the agency."

"She was kidding."

"Sure about that?"

"Yes," I said, although I believed the opposite.

"Ain't going to happen, Fran Green being the short side of an isosceles. Got something going here, you and me. Just beginning to gain traction with the business. Finding our rhythm, taking paychecks regularly, setting aside Ben Franklins for a rainy day. But the pie's too small to slice three ways."

"I have no intention of—"

Fran's voice rose. "I know you. You'd side with Destiny every time."

"Fran!"

"No offense. Love your honey. Wish she were mine most days."

My eyes narrowed. "You do?"

"But she ain't cut out for the kind of work we do."

"She isn't." I cast a guilty look at Destiny, who was about fifty feet away, outside, on a deck overlooking the community swimming pool. Through the open sliding glass door, I could see her engaged in conversation with Julianne Eaton, and I could hear children hooting and squealing in the distance.

"No, siree." Fran touched my chin and steered my head until I once again made eye contact with her. "Aims for the big picture, that girl. You and me, we deal in minutiae. She's go, go, go. We're laidback."

"We are?"

"She deals with projects. We deal with people. Have to level with you, kiddo. Bring her in, better buy me out."

"I never—"

"Got a friend who's a CPA. Could ask her to appraise the business. Pay me what's fair, and off I go, quietly into the sunset."

"Fran!"

Now she was the one who wouldn't meet my gaze. "What?"

"Shut up!"

She raised an eyebrow. "Come again?"

"Destiny's the executive director of the LCC. You and I are fifty-fifty partners in a private investigation firm. Nothing's changing."

"Ever?" she said, sneaking a look at me.

"Ever. If Destiny loses her job, God forbid—"

"God forbid!"

"—she'll find another one."

"Might not be possible. What if this fiasco follows her?"

"It won't, but even if it did, she could still find work in the private sector."

"In two shakes," Fran said, nodding. "But not in our private eye sector, right?"

"No."

"Promise?"

"I promise."

"Good. Puts my mind at ease." Fran pulled a large envelope from beneath her shirt and handed it to me in a furtive swoop. "Back to work. Eyeball this when you get a chance," she said out of the corner of her mouth.

"What is it?"

She pretended to brush something from my shoulder and spoke into my ear. "Photos, compliments of my teen operative at Roosevelt High."

"The cheerleader case," I said, mortified. "You didn't."

"Had to. That Chelsey's a natural at undercover work. Decent shutterbug, too."

"You had her take photos for you? Of what?"

"Jasmine Smith and Brittany Stallworth."

"No, no, no!"

Fran grinned. "Yep, yep, yep! Don't worry. Nothing racy."

"Jesus Christ," I muttered.

"Didn't stop there. Tracked down a copy of Jasmine Smith's work history, too."

"From Chelsey? Please!"

"Calm down. Tapped another source for that info." Fran made a dismissive motion. "But don't ask. Can't tell. Gotta go." She rose.

"Where?"

"Back to the house. Hate to miss this slugfest, but Destiny wants me to keep an eye on G. and T. Afraid they might do something rash."

"Wait." I grabbed her arm. "Take this picture back with you and ask Tracey if this guy looks like the man she and Kayla saw in the park."

Fran glanced at the photograph of Ken Bosworth. "Where'd you get this winner?"

"From Julianne Eaton's friend, Freddie Sampson. Freddie identified him as a likely threat to commit a child abduction. He lives three blocks from Kayla's house."

"Holy fruits!"

"Take this one, too." I thrust the mug shot of Todd Robie at her, face down.

She turned it over and let out a low whistle. "Who's this chain gang dude?"

"Freddie's second choice. He was released from prison ten days ago, and he now lives around the corner from Tracey and Gwen. Find out if they recognize him."

Fran's forehead wrinkled. "Will do. Call you later."

With that, Fran scurried off, and I was left to stare at her nine-by-twelve offering. I turned my shoulder to shield the envelope from the prying gaze of the woman at my elbow and anxiously pulled out a set of photographs and a stapled report marked "confidential."

The pictures were candid shots of Jasmine Smith and Brittany Stallworth, marked with today's date, Tuesday, September 18. Six in all, each was revealing. Nothing incriminating in the eyes of a court, but the snapshots plainly demonstrated an intimacy between the teacher and student. Their relationship was evident in the proprietary hand Ms. Smith put on Brittany's arm, also in the tilt of Brittany's head as she smiled at Ms. Smith.

I put the photos back in the envelope and began to read the report from St. Jude's school.

"A very caring person who wants to make a difference in young people's lives."

That was the prize line in the investigative file that Sister Mary John, the principal at St. Jude's, had opened on Jasmine Smith four years earlier.

"Jazz" had made a difference all right, but not the kind any moral adult would have condoned. It appeared as if she'd operated openly, with scads of parents and teachers looking the other way or seeing what they wanted to see.

The file included interviews with students, teachers and faculty members.

My judgment after a few minutes of reading: Jasmine Smith was a practiced predator who never should have been allowed to hold a position of trust.

She'd worked at St. Jude's for nearly eight years, her stint beginning a short time after she earned her teaching degree from Metropolitan State College in Denver. She'd taught English and coached the girls basketball team to seven state championships, an achievement many parents noted in their comments.

Rumors had swirled, most generated and perpetuated by students, but Sister Mary John hadn't been able to confirm any. As it was, the nun's report read like a flattering living history until I paid closer mind to ominous inferences.

For instance, it concerned me that for periods of time, Smith had lived with two families who had girls attending St. Jude's. First, the family of Katie Mathers. Later, Carly Siegel. Katie's mother had described Jasmine Smith as "a kind, caring and helpful person." Both families had accepted her as a trusted friend, and both girls had become the subject of school gossip.

In fact, Sister Mary John had opened the investigation after a student reported seeing Jasmine Smith and Carly Siegel together early one Saturday morning. The following Monday, when the principal confronted Smith, she admitted that she'd been with the fifteen-year-old girl. She explained that she was working with Carly on personal issues—counseling her for an eating disorder—and that they'd needed a private place to talk.

The back seat of Smith's van, according to the student who had caught them behind the school's maintenance shed.

Jasmine Smith acknowledged that the behavior might be perceived as inappropriate, and she asked Sister Mary John if the encounter was illegal. The nun assured her that it wasn't, but she began an inquiry, closing it two weeks later with one word.

Inconclusive.

Jasmine Smith had taught and coached at St. Jude's for another two years before applying at Roosevelt High School.

CHAPTER 17

A vibration on my leg startled me, and as quickly as I could, I reached into my pocket, retrieved my cell, flipped it open and read the text message from Fran.

Showed photos to G and T. Never seen skanky. Clean-cut's a dead ringer for park man. What now?

Good question.

"If I could have your attention, please," Suzanne Kemke called out as I was sending a text back to Fran, instructing her not to give Gwen or Tracey any information about Ken Bosworth. In their anguish, I was afraid of what one of them might do to a man convicted of ten counts of child abuse.

I closed my phone and looked up to see the president of the Meadowridge Homeowners' Association tapping a cordless microphone. The tall, thirty-something blonde wore stretch pants, a pink top and a rose-colored duster jacket. She'd pulled her hair back into a ponytail that stretched her skin. Heavy lipstick, liner and gloss exaggerated her oversized mouth, and when she spoke, her lips reminded me of a character in a Pixar film.

"We're going to go ahead and get started," Suzanne continued. "The purpose of this meeting is to raise awareness of measures we can take to keep our neighborhood and our children safe. With me tonight, we have Destiny Greaves, from a women's center. She was kind enough to arrange this meeting. She's been working closely with Kayla Martin's family. We also have Lieutenant Hillary Longhorn, who is our community liaison from the Highlands Ranch Police Department. She'll be providing safety tips. And Julianne Eaton is also here, a sexual abuse activist who works with local schools, neighborhood groups and HOA associations. She'll educate us about the sex offender registry—its strengths and weaknesses. We'll start by conveying some general information, after which, we'll open the discussion to include your questions or concerns. Lieutenant."

"Thank you, Suzanne," Lt. Longhorn said, stepping forward. She cleared her throat and looked down at the half-sheet of paper she held in front of her. "Folks, what I'm going to say tonight isn't anything new. Most of it is common sense, but it never hurts to review. I'll go through it, and you can ask specific questions afterward. Let's see . . ." She took a deep breath and cleared her throat again. "Don't leave your children unattended in public places. Make sure they know what to do if they become separated from you. Tell your children not to talk with strangers, especially if they're in parked or moving vehicles. Teach them to immediately report to you if a stranger contacts them. Identify safe people, neighbors your children can go to if they need help. Inform them that they shouldn't be afraid to make a scene, if they do feel unsafe." Hillary raised her head. "That goes for women, too. If something doesn't feel right, scream, yell, run. Don't try to please or accommodate someone. It's better to be embarrassed than to be seriously hurt."

The woman next to me made a grunting sound, and when I glanced over, she had her eyes half-closed, like a frog's.

I frowned at her before turning my attention back to Hillary. "Last item, for those of you with computer-literate children, monitor what they're doing online. We learned this summer that one of the social networking sites turned over seven thousand names and e-mail addresses of convicted sex offenders who had profiles on its site. The company did that only after being pressured by attorneys general from several states. The point being, predators are using the Internet to lure children, and law enforcement's always going to be one step behind. You need to be proactive about protecting your kids."

Hillary stepped to the side, and Julianne Eaton took her place.

"Most sexual assaults—on children and adults—are committed by someone the victim knows," Julianne said in a perky voice. "Eighty to ninety-five percent, according to recent figures. Strangers don't pose the highest risk. These statistics prove that. We also know that more than fifty percent of sex offenders re-offend, and that most offenders commit multiple crimes against multiple types of victims, across varied types of relationships. They rarely commit a crime impulsively. More typically, they plan carefully, which is part of the excitement for them. There is no such thing as an average sex offender. They come from all backgrounds, ages, income levels and professions. An offender might be sitting next to you at this very moment."

A few tittles of nervous laughter erupted, but otherwise, the audience seemed stunned into a hush.

"Why am I telling you this?" Julianne continued. "Because I'm the mother of four children, one of whom was on her way, two years ago, to meet a thirty-four-year-old married man she'd been chatting with on the Internet. Luckily, I caught her and stopped her. I know from firsthand experience how important it is that we pay attention to the people our children come into contact with, and the sex offender registry is one of the tools we can use to do that. It takes less than five minutes to check out a babysitter, neighbor, coach, caregiver or anyone who seems to be showing too much interest in your child. Every parent should take advantage of this valuable service."

Julianne started pacing slowly, from one side of the room to the other, her energy and enthusiasm similar to that of a motivational speaker. "Most law enforcement personnel believe that the registry provides some level of deterrent by letting these gentlemen know they're being watched. There are thirty-four sex offenders living in Highlands Ranch." Responding to loud gasps, she added calmly, "That might sound like a lot, but remember we're talking about a population of twenty-eight thousand people. If it's any consolation, there are two hundred and sixty-six living in District Six alone, the Denver Police Department district that encompasses the area east of downtown."

"That's why we don't live in Denver," a man shouted from the back of the room.

"And almost eight thousand convicted sex offenders are spread across Colorado," Julianne said, never acknowledging the interruption. "We've passed out information sheets with the Web addresses for the U.S. Department of Justice and the state of Colorado. Both of these sites are updated daily and contain information that includes the offender's name, address, date of birth, photograph and offense. Two notes of caution. Only offenders who have committed a felony sex crime or two or more misdemeanor sex crimes appear in these databases. Also, the Internet doesn't include names of juvenile offenders. Their names will be printed on a list at your local police station, so if you're concerned about someone, take the time to make that trip to your precinct headquarters. Another question I'm frequently asked concerns attempts. If you look on the sites, you'll see that many offenders were convicted of attempted sexual assault or attempted molestation or attempted sexual exploitation of a child. In most cases, that doesn't mean they tried something and failed partway. It means they pleaded to a lesser charge, which ninety-five percent of convicted offenders have done. Take away the word attempt, and you have a more realistic picture of the crime they, in truth, successfully completed. That's a capsulated description of how the system works. At this point, I'd like to open up the meeting to your questions."

Julianne pointed to a woman in the front row who was waving

her arm as if an insect were attached to it. "I heard on the news about a Web site that caters to sex offenders. Why can't you shut it down?"

Lieutenant Longhorn stepped forward. "For those of you who aren't familiar with this story, there's a business that gathers data from the registries and markets products and services to sex offenders. The business purports to connect offenders for purposes of living arrangements and jobs. There's nothing illegal about the venture."

"They're selling digital video recorders and wireless camera systems."

"I'm aware of that."

"That's bullshit," a man in a tie and sports coat said, his voice rising above the clamor from the crowd.

A woman by his side called out, "If most of these bad guys—I assume they're men—"

Julianne answered, "Ninety-six percent of sex offenders are male."

"—if most of them re-offend, it's obvious probation and registration aren't enough. Why can't they be incarcerated for life?"

"Because that would violate their constitutional rights."

"Send them to Alcatraz," a woman in front of me grumbled.

Suzanne Kemke intervened. "We're not here to debate the laws. We're here to come up with constructive solutions."

"It's a joke. Criminals have more rights than we do. What's the point?"

Hillary Longhorn stepped forward to say, "The system is working. Last month, police in Boulder arrested a sex offender for failing to register, and they found keys to twenty-one houses in his possession. Given the circumstances, there's a high likelihood Boulder officers prevented a crime."

Hillary pointed to a man in an HVAC uniform, who said with an edge to his voice, "Was that little girl abducted by a sex offender? I thought those two women she lived with had been arrested."

Destiny looked if she were about to explode, but she remained silent while Hillary fielded the question. "Gwen Martin and Tracey

Reid have been designated as persons of interest in our investigation, but no arrests have been made."

"Why not?" the HVAC man said.

"I can't comment on specifics, but we're working very methodically, actively pursuing all leads. Most of the work on the case has occurred outside the scope of the public and the media. That's all I can say."

A young woman in a baseball cap spoke up after Hillary nodded at her. "I was on the Colorado registry site earlier today, and in some areas, I saw especially high concentrations of offenders. Why is that?"

Hillary answered, "You might have been looking at a group home, a homeless shelter, or some type of low-income housing, such as a subsidized apartment building or trailer park. Many sex offenders have limited housing choices when they're released from prison."

An elderly man several chairs down from me didn't bother waiting his turn. He called out in an angry tone, "How can we get them out of our neighborhood?"

"You can't," Hillary replied. "They've served their time, and there's nothing you can do except educate yourselves as to their proximity."

"We ought to give them a taste of their own medicine."

Hillary's voice hardened. "The point of the registry was never to encourage retaliation or additional punishment. Any sort of vigilantism or violence toward an offender or his family will not be tolerated. We need to respect their rights. I can guarantee you that the department will aggressively investigate and prosecute individuals who act outside the constraints of the law."

"Why would you protect them?"

"Because, sir, we have a duty to protect the rights of all citizens, including sex offenders."

"I propose that we pass an HOA bylaw banning child molesters from living within twenty-five hundred feet of schools, school bus stops, day-care centers, parks or playgrounds. Miami Beach, Florida, did it. Why can't we?"

Suzanne responded, "Gene, that type of discussion might be more appropriate at our next scheduled HOA meeting, which will be the end of October. We'd love to have you there."

Julianne added, "Before you jump into anything, be aware that there are pros and cons to introducing sex-offender residency rules. For one, isolating offenders can push them underground, potentially making them more dangerous. If we force them out of every community, we'll drive them away from jobs, relatives and treatment programs. They'll live under bridges and in park restrooms, making it difficult to monitor them. Also, the idea of banning sex offenders gives you a false sense of security. We haven't seen any correlation with safety. You might prevent offenders from living in certain areas, but you can't bar them from being in an area. I would think long and hard before you consider this option. Tracking what's happened in other communities, I can guarantee that you'll have a protracted legal fight with the ACLU. You'll need deep reserves in your HOA budget for attorney fees to fight for something that has questionable value in protecting children."

Over the grumbling, a woman with a tight perm said loudly, "We've lived in Highlands Ranch for ten years, and it's been wonderful. But we've had more cops here in the last five days than we have in the last five years. It's frightening my children. They don't want to play outside, and they have friends who aren't allowed to visit our subdivision anymore. Everybody is uncomfortable with the situation. Is there an end in sight?"

Hillary replied, "I can't answer that, ma'am. We'll keep following the evidence until we find Kayla Martin. Right now, most of our investigation revolves around Meadowridge."

"We're hardworking, law-abiding, Christian people. Can we send our kids outside and feel safe?"

"There are no guarantees," Hillary said. "Not today. Not last month. Not next month."

"They could be living next door, down the street, near our playgrounds. You hear about these things, but we never thought it would happen here. The thought is chilling! Two homosexuals raising a child—that's the real crime."

Destiny broke the silence in the room by quietly saying, "Next question or comment."

CHAPTER 18

After the neighborhood meeting drew to a tense close, I gave Destiny a lingering kiss in the parking lot, and she climbed in her car and drove toward Pine Lane, where she intended to relieve Fran.

I headed for home, and shortly after I walked through the back door of our mansion apartment, I went to bed, but not to sleep. Try as I did, I couldn't block out all of the anger and fear from the past two hours, much less the accretion from recent days. I replayed snippets from the evening until the sights and sounds blurred into an incoherent mess. When the alarm went off at six, I could have sworn I hadn't slept a wink, except that my pillow was damp from drool.

I showered away my lethargy, dressed swiftly and arrived at the office by seven.

My first observation, upon seeing Fran, was that she looked as if she'd suffered the same or worse fate overnight. Slumped against the dry-erase board that hung in the front room of our office, she was drawing a line in slow motion, her cheek perilously close to the black ink. "Don't know how you do it," she said, barely stirring at my arrival.

"Do what?"

"Cope with the dark of night. Couldn't keep the lids closed last night. Kept popping open every hour. Wigged-out thoughts went through my head in the wee hours. Couldn't wait for dawn to break. Now the eyelids are five-pound weights, body feels like a semi hit it, stomach's doing flip-flops. Kill for a nap."

I threw my car keys on the desk and smiled. "Tell me about it. You've never had a restless night?"

"Not like this one."

"What kept you awake?"

"Bleak thoughts after my nighttime interview with Carly Siegel. No respite from the dark musings about Jasmine Smith. How about you? You sleep good?"

"Are you kidding? After that neighborhood meeting? Did Destiny tell you about it?"

Fran staggered to her desk and collapsed into her leather chair. "Briefing at the babysitting shift change, but love to hear your recap."

"It was a huge waste of time. All they did was terrify the neighbors."

"They who?"

I brushed crumbs from my chair and sat down with a thud. "Julianne Eaton and Hillary Longhorn."

Fran's eyebrows shot up. "Doesn't jibe with Destiny's version of events."

"Of course it doesn't," I said heatedly. "She's the one who organized the meeting. She'll never admit it, but nothing productive came from it. We're no closer to finding Kayla. Destiny might have thought she was doing something helpful, deflecting attention away from Gwen and Tracey, but she set a mob in motion."

"Bit of an exaggeration, no?"

"I'm not kidding. They're going after Todd Robie."

"Skanky man? Julianne leak his name?"

"She didn't, but one of the women at the meeting had been on the Internet, and she's obsessed with him. She's convinced that he took Kayla and every other missing child in America. She's crazy. The man next to me told me that she sits in her yard and pulls out blades of grass. Her lawn has hundreds of bare spots, but people listened to her as if she were an expert. Hillary kept stressing that no one should attack or harass Todd Robie, but every speaker ignored her. They want to post fliers exposing his past crimes. They tried to form a committee to buy the house he's renting. They plan on protesting on his street."

"Maybe we could send over the Christians," Fran said in a jovial manner.

"This isn't funny. People were irrational and angry. Most at Todd Robie, but some at Gwen and Tracey specifically, and lesbians in general. You should be glad you didn't have to sit through two hours of it."

"Didn't exactly have a barrel of laughs myself, kiddo. News copters buzzing overhead. Had to chase away teen hoodlums on bikes who tried to steal items from the shrine. Spent thirty minutes on the porch watching karate kid next door do her Kung Fu kicks. Moms were in separate beds by seven after a big fight."

"What did Gwen and Tracey argue about?"

"Couldn't say. Figured it was private. Left them alone in the master bedroom."

"Meaning you tried to eavesdrop, but weren't successful?"

Fran matched my smile. "TV was way up. Drowned out most of their words." She slapped herself on the forehead. "Before I forget, scheduled a four o'clock this p.m. with Katie Mathers. You mind flying solo on this one?"

"Katie Mathers? The girl I read about in the St. Jude's file?"

"One and the same. Bet you anything Katie and Jasmine Smith had something going. Inconclusive," she said with a sneer. "That school investigation was a farce."

"Last night, I take it Carly Siegel confirmed that she had an intimate relationship with Jasmine Smith?"

Fran tossed a manila folder onto my desk. "All in there. Read it and scream."

"You don't want to give me a verbal?"

"Not this time."

"You love to give verbal reports. Are you feeling okay?" I said, only partly in jest.

"In no mood." Fran cleared her throat. "Back to Mathers. Tracked her down. Got her coming to the office on the pretext we're freelance writers doing a piece on local b-ball stars who made it big in college. Think you can lay it on the line when she gets here, get her to spill the beans on Smith?"

"Do we have to do this now?"

"Gotta keep moving forward to get Brittany Stallworth out of the mess she's in. Can I count on you?"

"I guess," I said reluctantly. "But I wish you would do the interview with Katie Mathers. This is your case."

Fran stood, sighed and shook her head. "Can't. Thought I could, can't."

I studied her with concern. "Is something wrong?"

Her cheeks reddened, and she wouldn't meet my gaze. "Can't talk about it just yet. Appreciate the favor, you cutting me some slack."

"Of course, but—"

"Gotta run to the can," Fran said, hurrying down the hall. "Back in a jiff."

I sat there, dumfounded, uncertain whether to follow Fran or give her leeway.

The ringing phone made my decision for me.

I answered the third call that morning from Destiny, and she skipped all pleasantries this time around. "Those fucking police! I swear to God they've guaranteed that we'll never find Kayla."

"How so?" I said calmly.

"After their press conference, which essentially convicted Gwen and Tracey, the donations have stopped coming in."

"Slowed down?"

"One, Kris. One call since noon yesterday. A seventy-year-old lady from Vail wants to come down for the search on Saturday, which I've already canceled. My press conference had no impact. None whatsoever! Either no one saw it, or no one believed me. Now what will I tell Gwen and Tracey?"

"About what?"

"Their legal fees and household bills. I promised them that they wouldn't have to worry, that the community would take care of them."

"You gave your word?"

"Yes, but that's when it looked like I had thousands of lesbians backing me up," Destiny said defensively. "Now we're going to have to pay for everything out of our personal funds. Tens of thousands of dollars."

"Our money?" My voice cracked. "Yours and mine?"

"What else can we do? How would you feel if this were us, in the middle of a crisis, and we were being attacked from every angle?"

"Hopefully, it'll be over soon. Did anything useful come in on the tip line last night?"

Destiny snorted. "That tip line's a pain in the ass. Last night must have been a full moon. Three psychics called. One saw Kayla bleeding in a bathtub. Another swears she's buried in a field, near a popular hiking trail. The third one claims Kayla stopped breathing and turned blue. Why are they wasting our time?"

"They probably think they're being helpful."

"Or maybe they want to take a wild guess and win the fifty thousand in reward money. You'd think we were running a contest. I called about something else, though. I hope you don't mind, but I set up a meeting for you at nine o'clock, at forty-nine hundred Morrison Road. With Zoe Walter."

I jotted the address on a Post-it. "Who is she?"

"A spokeswoman for Tri-County Department of Human Services.

She used to work as a counselor at one of the group homes Tracey lived in when she was a teenager."

"I thought you didn't want us investigating Tracey."

"I don't. Zoe's on Tracey's side."

"She called the tip line?"

"She contacted me directly. She's been a supporter of the Center since I opened it. We dated briefly. Hello? Kris, are you there?" Destiny said after I didn't comment.

"Yes," I grunted.

"It was only two or three times, years ago."

"Do you still have feelings for her?"

"I never did. Could you please meet with her and find out if she has any insight that might help?"

"Mmm."

"We can't argue about this, Kris. You know I dated a lot of women before I met you. You know they're occasionally going to come back into our lives. Could we focus on Kayla and Gwen and Tracey?"

"All right," I said, gradually exiting my funk. "Did Hillary give Freddie Sampson's information to the investigators?"

"Yes, but it didn't do any good. Hillary doesn't think the detective in charge of the investigation will do anything with the sex offender profiles."

"Why?"

"Because the police chief is convinced that Tracey accidentally killed Kayla."

"Then what?"

"Disposed of her body."

"How? When?"

"Before she made the nine-one-one call. Hours or even days before."

"Days would mean Gwen helped Tracey with the cover-up."

"Exactly. How absurd is that? Gwen goes out looking for Kayla every day. Is that an act? The police are pricks."

"How did Tracey kill her? Has the police chief decided that, too?"

"Hillary told me that he floated a new theory at their morning briefing," Destiny said gloomily. "Tracey gave Kayla too much cold medication, and she never woke up from her nap. She died from an accidental overdose."

CHAPTER 19

Fran's return from the bathroom coincided with the end of my phone call with Destiny.

She walked toward the board on the wall, stood to the side of it and pointed with a laser I'd given her for her birthday.

I looked at her closely. "Are you okay?"

"Our kidnapper or killer's on this board," she said in a gruff voice. "Mark my words."

I tried to follow the red dot as it raced in a swirling pattern across black, smeared scrawls. "I can't even read your words."

She turned for a moment, and I could see her eyes were puffy. "Family. Neighbors. Colleagues. Acquaintances. Prowlers. Sex offenders. Co-workers. Any more categories?"

"This is overwhelming."

She stood tall. "Forget the categories for a sec. Take our top five suspects overall. Work our way out from there. Go!"

"My top five? Tracey. Gwen. Todd Robie and Ken Bosworth. Some other sex offender we haven't identified yet. And Bruce McCarthy. Whoops, that's six."

"Not a problem. Give you the one extra this one time."

"Are those yours, too?"

Fran fixed the laser on a box in the bottom right corner. "Agree with you on the daddy track, but no other overlap. My mind's going along the lines of Grandma Martin, religious zealot, well-meaning stranger or neighbor and neighbor-slash-sex offender."

I shook my head. "You lost me."

"Had a lot of time to ponder, what with the sleepless hours racking up. Lay this on your brain. Motive, means, opportunity," Fran said dramatically.

"What?"

"Grandma Martin snatched Kayla so she could raise her in a hetero environment. Came in the back door. Easy as pie."

"Gwen's mother had never met Kayla. She wasn't part of her life or Gwen's."

Fran scratched her head. "Point taken. How about religious zealot? Doesn't approve of dykes raising tykes. Came by, found Kayla wandering outside. Shepherded her off to the promised land."

"That sounds even more far-fetched."

"Moving on. Well-meaning stranger or neighbor. Came across Kayla meandering. Meant to do a good deed. Retrieved the little girl, but then couldn't part with her immediately. More time went by, more trouble for the Samaritan."

"I don't know," I said, doubt coating my tone. "What's the next one, neighbor-slash-sex offender?"

"Neighbor who offends, but's never been caught. Stroke of genius came to me at four in the a.m. Made more sense than a registered con striking on his own patch. You feel me?"

I shrugged. "All of those scenarios seem much less likely than the most simple answer. You don't believe Gwen or Tracey might have killed Kayla accidentally?"

"Nah. Spent enough time around those two to tell neither one's a killer or conspirator. Might have made some mistakes long ago, but those gals are genuinely stunned by what's happened to them. Can't fake the emotions they're showing. Not well enough to fool Fran Green, human polygraph." Fran tapped her knuckle on the top left corner of the board. "Come to Papa."

"Bruce McCarthy. I agree," I said with enthusiasm. "He has to be considered a prime suspect."

"Or prime target. Last night, cuckoo thought rocked my world. Work with me here. What if Kayla's not the intended victim? Add G., T. or B. to the mix, and now we got ourselves a whole new world of suspects."

"Meaning someone's trying to hurt Gwen, Tracey or Bruce?"

"You got it."

My head started throbbing. "Whoever took Kayla wasn't going after her?"

"Not per se."

"It wasn't a random act?"

"No possible way." Fran began to pace back and forth frantically. "Here's the problem we got. Cops looking at the moms, but who's looking at their enemies?"

"No one."

"Only us. You and me, baby. We need to carry this sucker across the finish line on our backs." Fran came to an abrupt halt. "What about this? Baddie from the past's come back to haunt our suburban moms."

I frowned. "What the hell are you talking about?"

"Meth associates, dealers or users. ID theft gang, ringleaders or check-cashers."

"Tracey and Gwen have been clean for five years."

"So they say."

"You don't believe them?"

"Meth's a bugger to kick. But let's give 'em the benefit of the doubt. They been toeing the line, but that wouldn't prevent some joker from messing around in their lives. Kidnap for ransom. Take a crack at that angle."

"No one's contacted Gwen or Tracey."

"That we know of," Fran said, drawing out her words. "Gwen goes tooling around every day. Might be making a drop. How about I follow her next time she takes off?"

I scoffed. "You'll never get out of that cul-de-sac and neighborhood without her seeing you."

"Wait at the exit. Pick up the target from there."

"There are four or five ways out of Highlands Ranch."

Fran furrowed her brow. "Understood. Back to my original plan. Let me take on Daddy-B, re-interview him. Could be his queer games at straight bars have ruffled some feathers. Also, might take a swing at bumping into the old-man sex offender at the park. Didn't you tell me Tracey and Kayla usually saw that cracker Ken around the eleventh hour?"

"Sometime between eleven and noon. That's what Tracey recalls."

"Good deal. Count on me to case the green between oh-eleven and oh-twelve hundred hours. If the perv doesn't show, I'll flash around his photo. See if I can get any mums or nannies to corroborate Tracey's account of lurking." Fran sucked her teeth. "Let's meet back at the Ranch at noon sharp. Partake of some of the deli spread, have the gals go back through the list of everyone they've wronged. Sound right to you?"

"I guess."

"You got something else on your agenda?"

I rolled my eyes. "At nine o'clock, I'm meeting with one of Destiny's girlfriends."

Fran did a double-take. "Come again?"

"Zoe Walter, this social worker Destiny dated before we met. Just my luck, she was a counselor at one of Tracey's group homes."

"That'd be relevant how?"

"I have no idea. I'm following Destiny's directions. I'm trying to treat her like she's one of our clients, but it isn't easy. I hate having her tell me what to do!"

Fran stuck out her lips. "Go along with it. Might lead to something."

"Do I have to?" I said, suddenly feeling depressed.

"After that, why don't you swing by the LCC and peruse the tip line leads one more time?"

"Again," I whined. "How many times do I have to read about bags and sacks, with logos, emblems and insignia? There's nothing useful in those notebooks of tips."

"Seems like it now, but never know what nugget of info's hidden in the pile of—"

"Crap! Pile of crap! That's all it is. People call the tip line because they're sitting at home in the middle of the day, with nothing else to do. Between commercials for whiplash lawyers and trade schools, they call the tip line."

"Better idea? Speak up."

"Why are we doing all of this anyway? Is Kayla alive? Do we have any chance of finding her?"

"Yep and yep."

"How can you sound so certain?"

Fran stared at me levelly. "Refuse to consider the alternative. Simple as that."

"It's like watching someone you love be buried alive."

"Excuse me?" I said, unable to absorb anything other than Zoe Walter's appearance.

This woman in her sixties didn't seem like Destiny's type. She had deep-set eyes, pronounced crow's feet and a patchwork of liver spots across her hands and face. When she'd greeted me, with a firm handshake and endearing smile, I'd been taken aback by her age and the color and disarray of her hair. Cut in a Florence Henderson style, patches of the orange-burgundy locks seemed to be missing. Zoe wore a loose blouse, long skirt and Birkenstocks, the same garb she'd donned in a photo on her desk. In the picture, she was accepting a dreamcatcher from a woman dressed in a Native American ceremonial outfit. Other personal photographs were displayed on the walls and shelves in the small, beige, windowless room, but none seemed to depict children or a life partner. In most, she posed alone.

"That's how a spouse once described to me how it felt to cope with her husband's addiction to meth," Zoe said in a soft tone. "The drug corrodes the part of the brain that facilitates day-to-day decision-making and impulse control. It also provides instant gratification and a sense of euphoria. It's cheaper than cocaine, and the high lasts longer, which is why the addiction rate has reached epidemic proportions."

I shifted in my seat, trying to get comfortable in the rolling chair. "Mmm."

"Some users function normally and don't require treatment for years. They hold high-level jobs, raise children and contribute to society. More typically, however, there's no shallow end of the pool. Unlike marijuana or alcohol, there's no safe way to test the water. The interesting aspect of meth, from a purely clinical point of view, is that it doesn't discriminate. It's found in every socio-economic circle, from inner-city ghettos to gated communities. Dealers can easily penetrate and decimate entire communities."

"Given the typical outcome, what's the appeal?"

"Studies have shown that users—and Tracey Reid certainly fits this profile—are likely to have experienced emotional, physical or sexual abuse as a child. The drug helps them cope with trauma by taking away emotional pain. However, it leaves in its place anxiety, aggression and a propensity for sudden violence."

"When you knew Tracey as a teenager, at the group home where you worked, was she violent?"

"I wouldn't have classified her as such, no. I recall that she was distant and disengaged, but not violent."

"She has an assault charge on her juvenile record."

Zoe smiled indulgently. "That's not uncommon. Violence is an unfortunate byproduct in many youth facilities. Incidents occur on a regular basis, but most are resolved internally. On occasion, a resident or staff member will insist on pressing charges, and the police are called in. Charges generally are expunged when the youth turns eighteen."

"When was the last time you had contact with Tracey?"

"I believe she was sixteen or seventeen."

"Ten or eleven years ago?"

"Approximately."

"Yet you called Destiny to vouch for her?"

Again Zoe flashed a smile. "Destiny may have misunderstood my intentions. I phoned to offer insight. Until you informed me that Tracey had struggled with an addiction to meth, I was unaware of the full circumstances surrounding the case."

"That puts your impressions of Tracey in a different light?"

"Unfortunately, yes," she said without hesitation.

"And changes your opinion of what might have happened to Kayla?"

She paused. "Possibly. Substance addiction certainly can overpower the bond between mother and child."

"Meaning?"

"Addicted mothers often put themselves before their children, leaving them vulnerable. It's not uncommon for mothers to forget or neglect their babies. To leave them in the bathtub. To take them along when they're buying or selling drugs. To injure them accidentally."

"If Tracey had started using meth again, would you have considered Kayla at risk?"

Zoe nodded gravely. "Profound."

"Does anyone break free for good?"

"Rarely. Relapse is part of the process, certainly to be expected. Breaking the cycle of addiction, even temporarily, requires mental health support, structured after-treatment support, family and friend support, community and societal support. Staying clean requires a concerted, multipronged effort."

"Would it have helped or hurt that Tracey's partner Gwen is also a recovered meth addict?"

"Recovering. Never recovered," Zoe corrected. "Helped, ideally." She arched both eyebrows. "Let me qualify that. *If* both women stayed clean. Otherwise, Gwen's involvement would have damaged Tracey's recovery, possibly enabled a relapse."

"Gwen and Tracey both claim they haven't used in five years, since they completed rehab together. How would I know if they're lying?"

"You probably wouldn't. I'd be particularly concerned for them now, due to the stress they're under."

"With the world watching, they might turn to meth?" I said doubtfully.

"It's not out of the question. As I mentioned earlier, the hallmark of the drug is that it allows users to tolerate intolerable situations."

I shook my head. "I would have noticed something."

"Not necessarily," Zoe Walter said, almost pityingly. "Meth addicts are master manipulators."

CHAPTER 20

At 8956 South Pine Lane, I found Fran on the front porch, in a wicker chair, her feet propped on its mate, her eyes pressed against a $3,000 pair of binoculars she'd bought on eBay for $450. A can of Coke and family-size bag of Ruffles sat on the round table next to her.

"No news, bad news, worse news," she called out as I trudged up the driveway. "Which you want first?"

"No news."

"No sign of Bruce McCarthy. Checked with people in the Clock Tower. Wasn't in his office yesterday or day before. Swung by the mansion. Couldn't rouse any neighbors."

I moved her feet and sat across from her, my back to the protestors. "What's the bad news?"

"No sign of Ken Bosworth, old-man sex offender, at the park.

Must have gone underground with the wave of publicity."

"Could anyone at the park verify Tracey's sightings?"

Fran lowered the field glasses. "Not a soul in sight. No wee ones, mums, dads, nannies, day-care providers. Place was a ghost town."

"That's odd." I turned around abruptly. "Where are the Pride Riders?"

After a long swig of soda, she answered, "No shows."

"No one came this morning?"

"One." She suppressed a belch. "Roared off soon as she saw she was the only one here. Tides are turning, and not in our favor. Christians doubled their ranks." She gestured at the swarm marching back and forth, seventy feet from us. "Overheard a confab. Another busload's due in at two."

"I can't wait," I said, resorting to sarcasm. "What's your worse news?"

"That was it. You get anywhere with the tip line leads?"

"No," I said, not bothering to divulge that I'd skimmed them.

"How about Destiny's ex-fling?"

"Zoe Walter thinks Gwen or Tracey or both could be using again, and we wouldn't know it."

Fran wrinkled her nose. "Impossible. What's she take us for? Rubes who were born yesterday and fell off the turnip truck?"

I shrugged and reached for the can of Coke. "What're Gwen and Tracey doing?" I said after I took a sip.

"G-woman's inside, at the dining room table, last I checked. T-woman's out and about." Fran pulled a chip from the bag and chomped on it loudly.

I looked at her in alarm. "Tracey's missing?"

Fran wiped her hand on her navy blue shirt, below the words, *Live Urgently*. "Not missing. Out and about. Beautiful day, ain't it? Blue sky. No clouds. Crisp temperature. Autumn splendor."

"Where'd she go?" I cut in.

"Couldn't say. Left before I arrived. Shortly after Destiny departed, best I can tell."

"Tracey's been gone since before eight o'clock? Five hours?"

"Thereabouts."

"Has anyone been in touch with her?"

"Gwen's called the cell a few times. Radio silence."

I slapped her knee. "Why doesn't this concern you?"

"After the knock-down, drag-out those two had last night, little space'll do 'em good. G. says T. likes to frequent Chatfield State Park. Partial to the Plum Creek trail. Fresh air and exercise might be just what the doctor ordered."

"Fran," I said deliberately, "Tracey hasn't left the house since last Thursday."

"Not true. Came to the search on Sunday. Saw her with my own eyeballs."

"Other than that," I amended. "She hasn't been alone since Kayla went missing."

Fran scratched her head. "Not at all?"

"No."

"Dang. Put it like that, cause for alarm. What do we do?"

"Keep trying her cell phone," I said, rising. "I'll go talk to Gwen."

I would never again view Gwen Martin in the same light.

Instead of seeing a loving mother dressed in a white turtleneck, blue cardigan and plus-size jeans, I saw a half-naked meth addict, running around like a madwoman, capable of doing anything for the next high.

Relapse. Master manipulator. Repetitive movements and jerks. Stunted brain. Intense addiction. No shallow end.

The eddy of Zoe Walter's words filled my head as I struggled to pay attention to Gwen's.

"A colleague introduced me to meth. He said it would help us meet a project deadline, and he was right. Every time I smoked meth, I had extra energy and confidence. I could accomplish an unbelievable amount of coding in short periods of time, volumes of work. I lost weight, and I loved the way I looked. I went from one-eighty to one-thirty in three months, and I was thrilled. I thought meth was the greatest drug ever invented. Instant gratification, with these highs that would last eight to twelve hours."

Seated at the head of the dining room table, Gwen was dwarfed by piles of cards, flowers and gift baskets that Destiny, Fran and I had brought over from the Lesbian Community Center in the days immediately following Kayla's disappearance. Since the police chief had held his press conference, we hadn't added anything—a fact that, mercifully, seemed to have escaped Gwen's notice.

"At first, I planned to use only on weekends or when a big project was due, but I couldn't control it. I found out too late that no one can. It was part of the high-tech environment, part of the social network. It seemed normal, but the drug lies to you. It makes you believe everything's okay when nothing is, and it makes you lie. I was living a split life, with two personalities. Gwen Martin, software engineer, high achiever, respected team leader. And Gwen Martin, drug addict, big loser, tweaker. I thought I had my two lives under control, but they collided."

"What made you go into rehab?"

She put her hand to her cheek. "I saw one of my co-workers try to cut out his own intestines. We were working late one night, using meth to plow through code. He'd already dismantled a VCR, and we thought that was hilarious . . ." her voice trailed off.

"Did he survive?"

"For three days. After he died, the owner of the company paid for five of us to go into rehab. He'd suspected what was going on, but he'd tolerated our quirks, as he called them, because we were productive. I voluntarily checked into the facility where I met Tracey. I spent the next three months sitting on rubber furniture, underneath fluorescent lighting, writing in a journal and talking to doctors and counselors. The day I completed the program, I quit my old job."

"You had to leave that environment?"

"To have any chance of success, yes. Also, it was part of the vow I'd made to Tracey. We both agreed to leave behind everything connected with meth."

"Did she break that vow last Thursday?" I said softly.

Gwen looked surprised. "She shared that with you?"

"Not specifically. She only told me that she'd lied about something."

"She should have told me sooner," Gwen said crossly. "She should have told the police."

"What happened?"

"One of her meth friends came by Thursday morning. Marla Semper."

Marla Semper. The name on the storage locker that contained identity theft supplies. "Marla came to the house?"

Gwen nodded. "Tracey finally told me last night, and we had a huge fight. The worst one we've ever had. I screamed at her that this was all her fault. Kayla. The police. The invasion of privacy. The protestors. If she'd agreed to take a polygraph when the police asked last Thursday, none of the rest of this would have happened. We wouldn't be under attack."

"You refused a polygraph, too, didn't you?"

"What choice did I have? If I'd agreed, it would have looked as if Tracey had something to hide. Which it turns out she did," Gwen said lethargically.

"Did your fight last night turn physical?"

"No, but it probably would have if Fran hadn't been in the other room. I told Tracey she has to move out. I also told her that when Kayla comes back, she can't have any contact with her. I won't put my daughter at risk."

"Isn't Tracey in the process of adopting Kayla?"

"Nothing's been finalized. The law allowing unmarried couples to adopt each other's children only went into effect last month. We'd started filling out the paperwork, but Tracey has no rights. Not yet."

"Tracey is Kayla's primary caregiver," I said faintly.

"My position might sound harsh, but there are no gray areas when it comes to meth."

"Maybe that's what made Tracey lie to you in the first place."

"You're either clean and away from the lifestyle, or you're not."

"You don't think Tracey's using again, do you?"

"I don't know what to think."

"Why did Marla come by? Did Tracey say?"

"For money. Tracey gave her two hundred dollars out of our safe."

I had an uneasy feeling. "Did Marla meet Kayla?"

"Yes. They spent time together on the porch, the three of them. Tracey swore she never let Marla in the house, but what does it matter? Tracey lied to the police, and she lied to me. Having that information last week might have made the difference in whether my daughter lives or dies."

"You believe Marla might have been involved in Kayla's abduction?"

"Yes," Gwen said flatly.

"Have you called the police?"

"No, and I won't. I'm done cooperating with them. Finding out that Marla Semper came by would only give them more ammunition against me and Tracey."

"It could also give them a fresh avenue to explore."

Gwen shook her head. "I'm not saying a word. The police believe Tracey gave Kayla an overdose of Benadryl. That's their latest ludicrous guess. That's all they know how to do, guess! They don't have a clue where my daughter is or how she got there. I'm supposed to trust them? Tracey never would have given Kayla adult cold medication. We'd talked about it before, how other mothers give medicine to their kids to sedate them, how wrong that is. As mad as I am at Tracey right now—and I'm livid, absolutely livid—I believe her when she says she didn't harm Kayla and she doesn't know who did. That won't prevent one or both of us from being arrested, but I believe her."

"Which brings me to an awkward point," I said tentatively. "Destiny asked me to talk to you about your finances."

She shot me an apprehensive look. "What about them?"

"Who pays the bills and keeps track of your money? You or Tracey?"

"I do. For both of us. Why?"

"If you're arrested, we'll want to get you released as soon as possible. The judge will set bail, and you'll have to post bond."

"We have to come up with cash?"

"No, but you'll have to pledge assets to cover the full amount. A bail bondsman will put up the funds. Do you know what your net worth is, give or take?"

She let out a grunt. "It's probably negative."

"You owe more than you own?"

Gwen put her head in her hands and closed her eyes. "We don't have any equity in the house. Our cars are leased. We both have student loans. We owe so much on our credit cards, that I can barely make the minimum payments."

"Is there anyone who could help? Someone who might lend you money or put up an asset?"

She opened her eyes slowly. "No."

"Your family? If you show up for court dates, the bail money is returned in full. All you owe is the ten percent that the bondsman charges as his fee."

"I said no."

"You wouldn't be willing to ask your parents for help?"

"I'd rather sit in a cell."

"Okay." I took a deep breath. "At last count, about sixty thousand dollars had come into the fund Destiny set up for you."

"Not including the reward money?"

"No. That's in a separate account."

"Are donations still coming in?"

"Very few," I said levelly. "The response from the community has slacked off since the police held their press conference."

"Sixty thousand won't be enough if both Tracey and I are charged with murder, will it?"

"No, but we'll work something out."

"I don't even care at this point," she said bleakly, inclining her head toward the street. "I'd rather be almost anywhere else than here."

"I don't blame you." Hate-filled rhetoric from the Christian protestors could be heard from every room in the house.

Gwen's eyes widened, and without warning, she bolted from her chair and ran out the front door.

CHAPTER 21

With the sound of sirens piercing the air, I chased after Gwen as she ran down the street at full pace.

My legs were burning and my lungs were screaming, and I couldn't catch up to her until she stopped at the opening of Ridgeback Circle. An ambulance and two police cruisers, lights flashing, were parked in front of the house at the tip of the dead-end street.

"It's Kayla," Gwen said, collapsing to the sidewalk. "They've found my little girl!"

I knelt beside her and put my hands on her shoulders. "I don't think so, Gwen."

"She's dead!" she screeched. "She can't be dead!"

"The body's too big." I cast a furtive glance at the gurney the emergency medical technicians were wheeling out of the house. "His head's poking out, and he must be alive, the way they're rushing."

"You're lying!" she said, her head buried in her arms, her body shaking violently.

"Gwen, listen!" I helped her stand up. "Look! It's not Kayla."

A small cluster of people had gathered fifty feet from the ambulance. I led Gwen toward them, tightly holding her hand, supporting a good portion of her weight.

"What's going on?" I asked a slender woman who had three toddlers in tow.

The woman's eyes darted from me to Gwen, and back to me again, before she replied in a calm tone, "The sick fuck got what he deserved."

I had a hard time convincing Gwen to leave the scene.

She kept insisting that Kayla was inside the house, and it required considerable persuasion, plus an admonition from a police officer to get her to move.

We walked back toward her house, arm in arm. After I escorted her up to the master bedroom, I pulled Fran aside in the kitchen and filled her in on what had happened to the man I believed to be Todd Robie, the sex offender. I also told her what Gwen and I had discussed before she sprinted out of the house. "While I'm gone, I need you to run a background check."

Fran pulled a spiral notebook from the waistband of her jeans. "Good as done. Subject?"

"Marla Semper, and be discreet. Don't let Gwen catch you."

"Semper." Fran made a note. "Connected how?"

"She's one of Tracey's friends from her drug days."

"Ancient history?"

"Recent. Last Thursday morning, Marla came to the house and borrowed money from Tracey."

Fran chewed on the tip of her pencil. "Large sum?"

"Two hundred dollars."

"Any contact with Kayla?"

"Marla met Kayla, but Tracey wouldn't let her inside the house."

"Wouldn't have prevented this Semper-Fi from conducting a recon mission later in the day."

"Exactly."

"Dang! We turn this gem of a lead over to the coppers?"

"Not yet. Presumably, they're already pursuing Marla from another angle. She's the one who shared the storage locker with Tracey."

Fran nodded thoughtfully. "Mastermind behind an ID theft ring?"

"She might be." I glanced at the clock on the stove. "I have to get going, or I'll be late for my meeting with Katie Mathers. Don't let Gwen leave the house alone. If she insists on searching for Kayla, you drive her around."

"Will do."

"I'll be back as soon as I can," I said, turning to leave.

"Go easy on her, kiddo."

I did an about-face. "Katie? A sexual abuse victim? You know I will."

"First love's always the cruelest heartache," Fran said solemnly.

"Would you prefer to interview her?"

"No, ma'am." Fran's breath quickened. "Been there, done that."

Been there, done what?

Was Fran referring to the interview she'd conducted with Carly Siegel the night before or to some forbidden love long ago?

My cell phone rang as I walked down the driveway. "Where have you been? Why haven't you answered your phone?" Destiny said.

"I'll call you right back." I closed the phone and threaded my way through groups of protestors, trying not to touch any. A few minutes later, from the safety of my car, I whispered, "Someone beat up Todd Robie."

I heard a sharp intake of breath. "How do you know?"

I put the cell phone closer to my mouth and started the engine. "I saw an ambulance drive off with him in it."

"You're sure it was Todd Robie?"

"The address matched his, and the man on the stretcher looked like him. Sort of. His face was all bloody and distorted, so I couldn't tell for sure."

"Do Gwen and Tracey know about this?"

"Gwen does. She was with me. She heard the sirens and ran down the street, thinking it was Kayla."

"Oh, no! And Tracey?"

"She's not back yet."

"No one's seen her?"

"Not since she left this morning."

"This isn't good. Do you think Tracey might have attacked Todd Robie?"

"How could she know where he lives? She wasn't at the neighborhood meeting, and Fran only showed her his picture last night, nothing else."

"Maybe Tracey recognized him and somehow connected him to his house."

"She told Fran he didn't look familiar."

"She could have lied, Kris. Or she could have accessed the sex offender registry and looked up his address."

"The police took her computers."

"There are terminals in every public library."

"God, I hope this isn't what she's been doing for the last six hours," I said, exasperated. "How horrible would that be? If Tracey was innocent, but isn't anymore?"

"Could you blame her?"

"I could if Todd Robie never touched Kayla. What if we set something in motion at that meeting last night?"

"Don't you mean *me*, Kris? What if *I* set something in motion, and I didn't. Todd Robie molested at least a dozen little girls in public places, but I didn't say a word to the neighbors about his crimes. I had his complete file, including revolting information that was never made available to the public, and I refrained from revealing any of it."

"That didn't stop that crazy lady from speaking up."

"It's not my fault someone else found out about a convicted sex offender through a public registry. That's the risk Todd Robie took when he chose to use little girls for sexual gratification. I'm not about to apologize."

"I didn't say you should. Could you call Hillary and see what she knows? I've got to leave here in a few minutes."

"Where are you going?"

"Back to the office. I'm supposed to meet a young woman Fran thinks had a relationship with Jasmine Smith, the teacher we're investigating in our cheerleader case."

"You have to do that right now?"

"When else am I supposed to do it? Fran took the case last week, before Kayla went missing. We have to follow through."

"I can't believe you two are working on another case when we haven't found Kayla."

I checked my temper. "A high school student's having an affair with her thirty-five-year-old teacher," I said tersely. "How is that not important?"

"It's not life and death."

"It could be. One of the students Jasmine Smith preyed on was a fifteen-year-old she was supposed to be in counseling for suicidal thoughts, the same one I'm meeting at four."

"I'm sorry," Destiny said, sounding only slightly contrite. "I'm consumed by Kayla. She's all I care about. I can't let in anything else."

"We could be looking for Kayla for weeks, or even months. Fran and I have to resolve this other issue, too. We don't necessarily have to accept any new cases, but we have to finish this one."

"Why can't Fran take care of it? Why do you have to be there?"

"This morning, after Fran asked me to handle the interview, she ran to the bathroom in tears."

"Fran? Crying? Why didn't you say something earlier, when I called you?"

"She was sitting right there."

"You made her cry?"

"No, I didn't make her cry," I said, ever so slowly. "I didn't do anything. This older woman/younger girl abuse must be triggering something in her."

"Like what?"

"Guilt," I said eventually.

"Kris!"

"Is that so hard to fathom? That Fran had a sexual relationship with someone younger, sometime in the course of her thirty years as a nun?"

"How much younger?"

"How would I know? I'm making this up as I go along. She won't tell me anything."

"That's not like Fran to hold back. Do you want me to say something to her?"

"No! Don't tell her I mentioned it. She'll think we were talking about her."

"We are!"

"I know, but don't bring it up. I have to work with her every day. I don't want tension between us."

"I can't picture Fran doing anything inappropriate."

"Then what's going on?"

"Fran might have been the victim," Destiny said after a long pause.

CHAPTER 22

"I'm not a victim. Those other girls you're talking about might be victims, but I'm not. Anything that happened, I did to myself," Katie Mathers said, fifteen minutes into our circuitous conversation.

The moment the former St. Jude's student had arrived at the office, I'd quickly dispensed with the lie about writing a sports article and had come to the point, watching with concern as the color drained from her face.

I'd informed Katie, in general terms, about the principal's investigation at St. Jude's. I'd shown her the photos left in the cheerleader's camera in Vail, of a vagina which she seemed to recognize. And, without naming her, I'd expressed concern for Brittany Stallworth, Jasmine Smith's latest victim.

"I loved Jazz, and she loved me," Katie said mulishly. "It was fate."

I showed no reaction. "Fate?"

Katie sat motionless on the couch next to my desk, feet on the floor, legs together. She wore a flowered skirt, pink top, Stanford letter jacket and red high tops with no hose or socks. "She told me I was special, and she wanted to make my first experience enjoyable. She knew girls my own age wouldn't know what to do."

"How old were you when you became sexually involved with Ms. Smith?"

She refolded her hands in her lap. "Fourteen."

A tall, statuesque brunette, Katie Mathers was nearly identical in appearance to Carly Siegel and Brittany Stallworth, the other victims Fran had interviewed. All three had high cheekbones, clear complexions and straight hair that fell to their shoulders.

"Ms. Smith was your coach at St. Jude's?"

Katie tipped her head to the side. "Yes, but I met her before that. At one of her summer basketball camps."

"How old were you?"

"Twelve. She told me she liked the way I played. She said I had a lot of hustle and poise, and she wanted me to be on her year-round team. I was the youngest player. Some girls were as old as eighteen. She said I could be a star, and she helped me enroll at St. Jude's."

"Did she also help you obtain a scholarship and financial aid?" I asked, curious whether this part of Katie's history mirrored Carly Siegel's.

"Yes."

"When did Ms. Smith move in with your family?"

"Right before my fourteenth birthday. She was having work done on her house, and my parents told her she could stay with us."

"That's when your sexual relationship began?"

"Not right away," she said with a dispassionate air. "She lived in the basement, but she'd come upstairs to watch TV."

"Who initiated the physical contact?"

"Both of us." Katie's fingernails grazed the fabric of the couch. "After my parents went to bed, we'd cuddle and play around."

"Play around?"

Her tone became more lifeless. "She'd pretend to body slam me, and I'd punch her. She'd tickle me. We'd arm wrestle."

"When did the contact turn sexual?"

Katie wouldn't raise her head. "It was my fault. Jazz couldn't help herself. One day, she told me she was falling in love. She whispered it in my ear, and I begged her to make love to me. She finally agreed."

My stomach knotted. "With conditions?" I said, anxious to measure her account against Carly Siegel's.

Her nod was almost imperceptible. "She wanted to make sure I consented. She didn't want to force me into anything. She made me promise to keep the relationship a secret."

"Your parents weren't aware of any of this?"

"They said we shouldn't spend so much time together, but they didn't make us stop."

I rubbed my forehead. "I understand why you wouldn't want to go to the police. I also understand why you'd want to protect someone you care about. But would you feel differently if I told you that what you've described is identical to the pattern Ms. Smith used to seduce another girl, after you left for Stanford?"

Splotches surfaced on Katie's face, and her hands shook. "Who?"

I chose my words with care. "I can't disclose her name, but this might sound familiar. Ms. Smith gave the girl a cell phone and paid the bill. That allowed her to stay in touch and monitor the girl's calls. They spoke on the phone forty hours a week or more. They had sex, almost every day, for four years, beginning when the girl was fourteen. Ms. Smith told the girl she knew what they were doing was wrong, but that it felt right."

I wasn't hypothesizing.

I'd gleaned every word from the file Fran had left on my desk that morning, a summary of the interview she'd conducted with Carly Siegel the night before.

Katie's teeth began to chatter, but she didn't respond.

I continued, in a gentle but determined voice. "Ms. Smith and this girl had sex on the campus of St. Jude's—in the library, faculty lounge, classrooms, supply rooms, restrooms, janitor closets."

Katie let out a choking sound and tugged at the ends of her hair.

I felt dizzy, but I plowed forward. "Ms. Smith told the girl she wanted to live with her, but that they couldn't because of how it would look for a faculty member to become involved with a student. She convinced this student that they were practically married, as much as they could be. The two of them began with horseplay and progressed to fondling, which ultimately led to oral sex and sex toys. All the while, this young girl was seeing a therapist for an eating disorder, but she never had the courage to talk about Ms. Smith in counseling."

"I was addicted to alcohol and cocaine," Katie said in a disembodied voice.

"When it came time for the girl to graduate from high school, Ms. Smith persuaded her to attend the University of Tennessee, despite the girl's preference to stay in Colorado. That made room for Ms. Smith's next victim. A year ago, this girl I've been talking about confronted Ms. Smith and told her that she should have waited until she was older before they had sex. To that, Ms. Smith replied that the girl had always been old for her age."

Katie's eyes welled up, and she stiffened.

I broke the silence. "Ms. Smith told her that she loved her, only her, that she'd never done anything like this before. That if the girl went to the police, Ms. Smith would lose her job and go to jail. Ms. Smith went further, by threatening to kill herself if the girl exposed their relationship. Ms. Smith told the girl she cared for her very much and wanted her back."

"I felt safe with Jazz," Katie said at last, the ragged utterance giving way to weeping.

Two Tylenols did nothing for the splitting headache that grew as I typed up a summary of my interview with Katie.

I took two more pills, swallowing them with a sip of room-temperature water from a bottle on Fran's desk, finished the report and dragged myself to my car for the return trip to Highlands Ranch.

Kayla Martin had been missing for five days—only three of which had involved me—and it felt like five years. On the journey down Broadway Street, through bumper-to-bumper traffic, I began to long for a resolution.

Something to make it end.

"Kayla's been found!" Gwen called out brightly when I rejoined her and Fran in the living room of the Martin-Reid house at six o'clock.

I looked to Fran for confirmation, and she raised her shoulders in an exaggerated manner. "Twice."

My heart started pounding. "What do you mean?"

Gwen stared in the direction of the ceiling. "Thank God! Destiny told us a few minutes ago. Two promising calls came in to the tip line."

Fran stood, approached and hissed in my ear, "Rookie mistake. Giving the client info without corroboration."

"Friday, someone saw a woman at a bus stop in Denver with a girl who looked like Kayla, and the girl was crying." Gwen inhaled deeply. "And a woman in Littleton who's been trying to have a baby for years suddenly was seen with a girl fitting Kayla's description."

Fran said evenly, "Been counseling Gwen not to put too much stock in the reports."

"It feels right. This is the day. I wish Tracey were here. Any minute, I'll see my baby." Gwen jumped up and paced back and forth, her arms flailing. "I know the police have procedures to follow, but I want to hold her so badly. We'll go for a walk. Kayla loves to run up the street ahead of me, but she knows to stop at every corner. She holds out her hand and waits for me to catch up. She loves to swing at the park. She always chooses the one in the middle. I'll swing her for as long as she wants. We'll make chocolate chip cookies and watch *Scooby Doo*. She can sleep with me and Tracey in our bed. I've forgiven Tracey. We'll all be together. I can't wait! I'm out of my mind with joy. I knew Kayla was alive. No one believed me, but I knew."

Fran looked to me for direction, and I motioned for her to grab Gwen. "I'll be right back," I said curtly.

• • •

I ducked into the powder room on the main floor, locked the door and called Destiny.

"Why did you tell Gwen about the leads?"

"I couldn't help it. I blurted them out when I was talking to her. She sounded so down about Tracey being gone, I wanted to cheer her up."

"Destiny!" I said, a warning in my tone.

"I'm sorry. The instant I spoke, I knew I'd made a mistake."

"Three hundred tips about little blond girls have come into the tip line. Not to mention mysterious bags of clothing, bodies floating in canals and fresh mounds of dirt in backyards and parks. What makes these two leads any different?"

"They're specific, with detailed information that matches facts of the case."

"When will the police be able to verify or refute the accounts?"

"Probably not until tomorrow."

"Gwen has to wait in this frenzy until then?"

"She's excited?" Destiny said in a meek voice.

"That's putting it mildly."

"I screwed up, didn't I?"

"Royally."

"Do you want me to talk to her?"

"I'll handle it. I just wish you hadn't—"

"Hold on, Kris. That's my other line. It's Hillary."

"Go!"

The next sixty seconds were agonizing, and my spirits didn't improve when Destiny spoke again. "Hillary doesn't know anything more."

"Damn it!"

"She called to confirm that the man you and Gwen saw being loaded into the ambulance was Todd Robie. He died on the way to the hospital."

"No!" I groaned.

"Hillary wanted to make sure Gwen and Tracey have solid alibis."

"What did you tell her?"

"That I'd check with you and get back with her. Tracey hasn't come home yet?"

"No."

"No one's seen or heard from her since this morning?"

"Not as far as I know, but I'll double-check."

"Do! And call me back. Jesus Christ, Tracey better not have assaulted Robie. If she did, she went after the wrong sex offender."

"How do you know?"

"Hillary told me that detectives have traced his movements. Last Thursday, Robie was part of a day labor crew that worked from noon until eight, digging a ditch in Commerce City. He couldn't have abducted Kayla."

"Fuck!" I whispered, stretching out the word. "You know what this means?"

"Don't go there, Kris!"

"I told you we—"

"Hold on," she interrupted. "It's Hillary again."

"Let this be good news," I muttered while I waited. Seconds ticked away into minutes, and I was about to hang up and redial when Destiny came back on the line.

"The Westminster Police called the Highlands Ranch station."

I felt faint. "Did they find Kayla? Please tell me she's alive."

"They found Tracey."

"Oh, no!" My eyes welled up, a reaction to the distress in Destiny's voice. "Where?"

"Inside the rental car. In a parking lot at the Butterfly Pavilion."

"She's not alive?"

"No," Destiny said dully.

"Was she killed? Did she kill herself? Did she accidentally overdose?"

"Hillary doesn't have any details. A victim's advocate from Westminster is on her way to meet with Gwen, but could you do it?"

My voice shook. "Tell her?"

"Please!"

"Tell her that her daughter's still missing, and her life partner's dead?"

"Kris, please! Calm down! Fran's there, right?"

"Yes."

"Gwen trusts and respects both of you. Please, do this for me."

"I have to go," I said, slamming shut the cell phone.

Seconds later, I threw up, only making it to the toilet in time because I'd been sitting on it.

CHAPTER 23

"Kayla called it the insect zoo. Tracey took her to the Butterfly Pavilion every Wednesday morning, for Creepy Crawly Tales at eleven. After story hour, they'd walk through the exhibits and then go to lunch at McDonald's. They went every week."

"Amazing place, the Butterfly Pavilion," Fran said, pinching the bridge of her nose. "Been a few times myself. Take the out-of-town visitors whenever I get the chance. Tropical rainforest never fails to impress."

"I've never been. I can't go with them because I always have to work. That's all I do. Work. For what? To provide for my family, but I don't have a family anymore." Gwen looked at me. "She didn't suffer, did she?"

"Heart failure's generally swift and painless," Fran answered for me.

"How do they know it was a heart attack?"

"That's what the EMTs on the scene thought," I said, offering what little information Destiny had conveyed when she called back as I was rinsing my mouth in the bathroom. "They'll know for sure after the medical examiner's had a chance to look at her."

"I don't want her cut up."

Fran said, "Have to conduct an autopsy, Gwen."

"Can I see her?"

"Not yet," I answered.

"Where is she?"

"They took her to North Metro Hospital."

"Is she in a room?"

"No."

"Body'd be in the morgue," Fran added.

"Twelve hundred butterflies are loose in the tropical conservatory at the Pavilion. Kayla thought she'd seen every one of them," Gwen said with a distressed smile. "She named the turtles and frogs. She loved to touch the sea stars and horseshoe crabs in the water tank. My daughter's missing, you know."

Fran and I nodded.

"Everyone thinks I had something to do with her disappearance. That I hurt her or I'm covering up something."

"Not everyone," Fran said stoutly. "Me and Kris are in your corner."

"The police are coming to arrest me. I know they are. How will I make funeral arrangements if I'm in jail?"

"We'll take care of everything," I said, tightening my grip on her hand. Fran, Gwen and I were seated in a row on the couch in the living room. Fran had her arm around Gwen's shoulders, and I held Gwen's right hand.

Gwen used her other hand to dab at her eyes with a tissue Fran had provided from the box on her lap. "Kayla loved to hold Rosie the tarantula. She even kissed her," she said in the midst of a broken laugh. "Kayla might come home, right? If she does, I won't be arrested, and we can attend Tracey's funeral together. I'll wait for Kayla.

I won't bury Tracey until we're all together again."

"One day at a time," Fran advised.

"As soon as that woman on the bus brings back Kayla. Or the one who couldn't have children. Kayla's young. Whatever's happened, she can still have a happy life, right?"

"Absolutely," I said.

"That's all Tracey wanted. She bought Kayla a net and magnifying glass, and they started a butterfly garden out back. Did you see it? It's in the corner of the yard, behind the benches. Sunny but sheltered, with a mud puddle for the male butterflies. Did the police trample the flowers and shrubs yesterday? Is everything ruined? All the perennials and annuals? What will happen to the butterflies? They need the nectar and the host plants," Gwen cried, before slumping over and retreating into another round of sobs.

Over her head, I shot Fran a questioning look. She shrugged and said in a soothing voice, "Tracey and Kayla ever hike the nature loop outside the Pavilion? Love it myself."

Gwen nodded from her lap. "They do, too. They saw beavers and prairie dogs on the trail. Even a bald eagle once."

"Beautiful setting for a refuge," Fran murmured.

"I was mean to Tracey last night. I said hurtful things I shouldn't have. What if those were the last memories she had?"

"If she was at the Butterfly Pavilion—a place she loved—I'm sure she was remembering the great times she had with you and Kayla," I said as I rubbed Gwen's back. "The love you had for each other."

"People were saying such horrible things about her, people she thought were her friends. That she was a strict disciplinarian. That she was the man in the relationship. That she wanted Kayla to call her Daddy. Where did that come from?"

"Media twists the words," Fran said. "Uses sensational ones out of context."

"Tracey was so loving. She gave Kayla a bath every night. She'd shampoo her hair and swirl it into wild hairdos with funny names. The Pippi Longstocking. The Librarian Bun. Kayla would look at herself in a mirror and laugh and laugh. I could hear her from the kitchen. She loved Old Man Combover the most. And the Abe Lincoln sideburns Tracey made out of bubbles."

"Sounds like they had a lot of fun together," Fran said, a tear leaking out her left eye.

"No one understood her." Gwen straightened up and wiped the back of her hand across her nose. "All Tracey ever wanted was for her past to stop interfering with her future. Was that too much to ask?"

"Everyone deserves that much," I responded.

"When I first met her, she didn't think she was important, or that she'd ever be allowed to do anything. She didn't have any friends the first few years we were together. No one could bridge the gap between the two worlds she lived in." Gwen paused. "No one, except me."

"Two of you were as close as any couple," Fran said.

"The police asked me a thousand times, in a hundred different ways, if Tracey was using meth. She wasn't. She wouldn't have. She'd come too far to lose it all."

"Matter of course, they'll run tox screens. Prove Tracey was clean. Put the rumors to rest, once and for all," Fran offered.

"The police expected Tracey to run from the house screaming after she discovered Kayla wasn't in her bedroom. But Tracey wouldn't have," Gwen said desperately. "Would she? Not after what she'd been through, what she'd seen growing up. Her reaction was perfectly normal, for her! Why couldn't the police accept that and leave us alone?"

"Doing their job," Fran said. "And doing it poorly."

"Tracey loved Kayla to pieces. More than she loved herself. She never would have hurt her."

"I believe you," I said, my voice thick with emotion.

"I miss her so much." Gwen's head swiveled back and forth as she looked at Fran and me. "Promise me something."

"Whatever we can do," I said.

Fran chimed in, "Name it."

"Bring me back my daughter's body."

Before Fran or I could react to Gwen's plea, the doorbell rang.

• • •

I opened the front door to find Sierra Frazier standing on the porch. Dressed in leggings, a glittery shirt and a black skirt covered with tiny rhinestones, she touched the sunglasses on top of her head, as if to verify she hadn't lost them.

"Has Kayla come home yet?"

"Not yet."

"Can I come in and play in her room?"

"I don't think that's a good idea."

She picked through a baggie full of Lucky Charms and carefully placed a pink marshmallow on her tongue. "I won't take anything. I promise."

"Not now, Sierra."

"I brought everything back," she said plaintively, turning to point at the mound of toys and stuffed animals surrounding the mailbox.

"That's good. Maybe some other time."

"I know where Kayla is."

I peered at her intently. "Where?"

She shifted her weight from one foot to the other. "In heaven."

"Don't say that."

"Why is she crying?" Sierra said, reacting to the noise behind me.

I stepped outside and pulled the door closed. "Gwen? Because she feels sad."

The nine-year-old cocked her head and tugged on her hair. "I feel sad, too."

"About Kayla?"

Sierra nodded solemnly. "Want to play the hot-cold game?"

"What's that?"

"You hide something and then tell me if I'm getting hot or cold. Or I can hide something. Either way."

I smiled. "I love that game. I used to play it with my sisters when I was your age."

"Can we play? Can we, please? I'll let you go first."

"I can't," I said apologetically. "I have to spend time with

Gwen."

"She could play, too."

"She's not in the mood."

"Can I show you some of my kicks?"

"I don't know . . ."

"Grand Master Lee says we're only supposed to use martial arts for protection. He says if I can accomplish my black belt, I can accomplish anything. He wants me to do my best."

"Sierra, I have to—"

"My best day in my whole life," she interrupted, "was the day I earned my brown belt. June sixth. Now I'm in the black-belt club. That means I'm studying for it, but I don't have it yet."

"That's nice."

"I'm going to get my black belt before the other kids, even the older ones."

"Isn't it time for dinner?" I said, hoping she'd take the hint.

"I'm not eating dinner tonight. I'm too fat."

"You're not fat, and you should eat something."

"If I don't practice every day, I can't get the black belt."

"Couldn't you practice your kicks on your own, when no one's watching?"

Sierra's face fell. "Yeah, but—"

"That's what you'll have to do for now, because I need to get back inside."

"I could come with you," she said eagerly.

"Sierra, no!"

"Want to see my belts? I have them in my room, but I could bring them over."

"Not tonight," I said firmly, my hand on the doorknob. "I'll see you later."

"I remembered something."

"Good for you."

"Don't you want to know what it is?"

I refrained from sighing. "Sure."

"The day Kayla got lost, I saw a lady in a monkey-shoe car," Sierra called out over her shoulder as she skipped down the driveway. "After I came home from school."

"That was Sierra," I said to Fran and Gwen, who hadn't budged from the couch in the living room.

Gwen raised her head from Fran's lap. "Did you tell her to go away?"

"About ten times."

"I don't have the patience for her. I always try to send her home. Tracey does better with her."

"Does Sierra lie a lot?"

"Sometimes. Usually to get attention, but my main complaint is that she takes Kayla's toys without asking."

"Been bringing those back, little by little," Fran said to Gwen, before focusing on me. "She show you the karate moves?"

"She tried, but I wouldn't let her."

"Why you asking about the fibs?"

"I can't get a good read on her."

"She's starving for attention," Gwen said, sniffling. "Her dad moved out, and her mom works long hours. The only relationship Kim and Sierra have is through that ridiculous Webcam."

Fran continued to stroke Gwen's hair. "Sierra see something she's not telling you about?"

"Or told me about something she didn't see," I said pensively. "A lady in a monkey-shoe car."

"What's up with that?"

"Who knows? Do you want to try to interview her?"

"Not at this juncture." Fran gestured helplessly above Gwen's head, out of range of her sight. "Maybe later. That your phone ringing?"

"Yes," I said, patting my pockets frantically.

"Last I saw it, on the kitchen island. Next to the chips. Bring me a Coke on your way back, would you?"

• • •

In the kitchen, between the fourth and fifth ring, I pressed the talk button and caught Destiny's call before it went to voice mail. "Hey."

"Hillary called to tell me they know who killed Todd Robie."

"Please tell me they're not coming to arrest Gwen," I said in an urgent whisper.

"No, and Tracey didn't attack him either."

"Thank God!"

"He was killed by a fifteen-year-old boy who lives in the house behind Robie's."

"Fifteen?"

"The boy's parents turned him in earlier this afternoon. After his mom found a bloody baseball bat in his bedroom."

"Had Todd Robie—"

"Molested him?" Destiny completed my sentence. "No. The boy said they'd never met."

"Then why—"

"An older cousin had been sexually assaulting him."

"The boy never told his parents?"

"If he did, they didn't do anything to stop it."

"How did he know about Robie? Did he go online to the registry?"

"No." There was a long pause. "He overheard his parents talking after the neighborhood meeting."

"That couldn't have set him off. Not that alone."

"He thought he was helping, Kris," Destiny said, a catch in her voice. "After he came home from school, he picked up his bat and went to Robie's house. He knocked on the door, was invited in and beat the man to death—to save other boys. That's what he told the detectives who interviewed him. Somehow, he twisted everything in his mind."

"Or maybe, he knew exactly what he was doing. Someone's at the door," I said hurriedly. "I'll call you right back."

CHAPTER 24

"In the future, I'd appreciate it if when Sierra comes over, you'd send her home immediately," Kim Frazier said, before I could utter a word.

"I tried."

"The atmosphere over here isn't healthy," she said, seeming not to have heard me.

"I heard you."

She ran a hand through blond hair that curled around her neck. "Between the police searches and the protestors and all the comings and goings, it's having a terrible effect on my daughter."

"I understand."

"She's at an impressionable age."

"Okay."

"It has nothing to do with guilt or innocence or one chosen

lifestyle or another. I simply want to protect my daughter."

"I get it," I said, losing the last vestiges of patience.

"She's been through too much already. Sierra was fragile before—" Kim broke off.

I stared at her inquisitively. "Before Kayla went missing?"

Sierra's mother nodded. "Once she found out my husband and I were divorcing, she practically moved in over here. It wasn't productive. I tried to limit her time with Kayla, but it's been hard on her, the separation."

"This week's been hard on everyone," I said pointedly.

"Sierra's fixated on Kayla. She hasn't done her homework this week. She won't talk to her friends. She hasn't touched her phone."

"Hopefully, we'll have a resolution soon."

"Yes," Kim said vaguely. She turned to leave, adding as an apparent afterthought, "Tell Gwen I'm sorry."

I took refuge in the powder room and hit redial. "I'm back."

"Who was at the door?" Destiny said.

"Kim Frazier, the next-door neighbor. Has Tracey's death hit the news?"

"It must have. Wren Priestly just e-mailed me. I give up."

"On what?"

"Wren Priestly. My job. The Center. The lesbian community. I'm sick of it all!"

"Wren pulled the reward?"

"Ten minutes ago, and she was too much of a coward to do it herself. She had her assistant write three lines of bullshit about the disappearance of Kayla Martin no longer aligning with the goals and values of the United Lesbian Foundation."

"Have you responded?"

"Yes, with a suck-up reply saying I understand Wren's position, but hope she'll reconsider."

"You couldn't tell her to fuck off?"

"No, Kris," Destiny said bitterly. "We have six projects we're working on with her foundation. I can't put them at risk. Have I made the biggest mistake of my life?"

"I hope not."

"Is all this for nothing? Is Kayla dead?"

"You can't think about that."

"Did Tracey do it?"

"Destiny!"

"Did Gwen help Tracey hide the body?"

"This isn't helping."

"Will I still have a job if I was wrong about supporting the two of them?"

"Of course you will!"

"At least I have a fallback. Working with you and Fran," she said, sounding as lukewarm as I felt.

"You won't need a Plan B."

"We could have fun together."

"Mmm," I said, too frayed for pretense.

"Did you talk to Fran? Was she excited about the possibility?"

"We didn't have a chance to go into any detail."

"Is she still at the house?"

"She's in the living room comforting Gwen."

"Good. Tell Gwen I'll get there as soon as I can."

"You don't have to come tonight. Fran's offered to stay over."

"I want to come. I'll see you in an hour or so."

"No. I have to leave in five minutes. I have an appointment with a detective in Denver, for that position of trust case Fran and I are working. I'm turning over the information we've gathered."

"All right. Call me when you're finished with your meeting. That's my other line," Destiny said. "I've got to run. Before I forget, though, when you get home tonight, could you pull out that financial statement we filled out in the spring?"

"Okay," I said warily.

"I want to know where we're at, to see if we can replace the fifty thousand Wren just pulled."

"Fifty thousand? Us? By ourselves?"

"In the morning, you can go by the bank and find out what we need to do to get a line of credit on the house."

I bit my lip. "Do I have to?"

"Please, Kris! I'll sign whatever paperwork's necessary, but I can't handle one more thing right now."

"I'll take care of it," I said, sighing heavily.

Screw Wells Fargo.

I went into the other room and asked to see Fran for a minute, in private, explaining to Gwen that I had a question about another case we were working.

Fran detangled her limbs from Gwen's body and joined me in the bathroom, where I furnished a condensed update.

"Lose that reward," she said, her brow wrinkling, "lose the best chance of a positive result."

"I know. That's why Destiny wants us to put up the money."

"Bad idea. Leave it to me."

"What will you do?"

"Got to be smart about this. Operation Greenmail," Fran said, rubbing her hands together.

I wrung mine. "Is that similar to blackmail?"

"Same deal, more scruples. That Wrench keeps a low profile, almost incognito. Strike you as odd?"

"If I were worth more than a hundred million, I wouldn't advertise it either."

"Particularly," Fran said with relish, "if your finances were iffy."

I threw up my hands in confusion. "Wren Priestly doesn't have a high net worth?"

"Sky high. Matter of public record." Fran wriggled her eyebrows. "But where did the funds come from to fund the company that funded the foundation that funds LGBTI causes? I get those initials right?"

"Close enough."

"The powers-that-be add something in there recently? Asexual?

Questioning? LGBTIAQ? Can't keep up with all the politically correct versions."

"Whatever," I said irritably. "Could you focus on Wren?"

"Like a laser. Heard a rumor years ago, never gave it much thought. Malfeasance and the like. Big word like that made me yawn before I got into the private eye profession."

"You know something?" I said, suddenly animated.

"Nothing specific. Let me put out some feelers. See what I come up with. Forty-eight hours, tops. Have something by then, or we move on."

"You're sure you want to do this?"

"Love to!" Fran smiled broadly. "Wren Priestly wants to judge our girls, better get ready to be judged herself."

Leaving the house, I saw a woman with a Westminster Police Department identity badge climbing out of a white Ford Taurus.

Presumably, she was the victim's advocate, dispatched to bear the news Gwen Martin already had bore.

I quickened my pace, eager to be as far away from the reverberations of grief as possible.

When I reached my car, however, it dawned on me that I should slow down.

The lower my miles per hour, the longer it would take to arrive at the District Six police station on Colfax and Clarkson.

Was it really such a big deal, I debated as I drove down Broadway, if a teenage girl had a crush on her high school teacher and the teacher encouraged the flirtations?

I was less than a mile from my destination when reality struck, and I flashed on the images stored in a teenager's camera.

Teachers should *not* be photographing their vaginas and sharing the snapshots with their students.

Without question, that was wrong.

How wrong?

I'd leave that up to law enforcement personnel to decide.

• • •

In some form of a modern-day wonder, I slept deeply that night, only stirring at the sound of the first alarm.

Three snooze buttons later, I rose, showered and grabbed two pieces of fruit on my way out the door.

In the parking garage of the Wells Fargo branch in Cherry Creek, I downed a breath mint to mitigate banana breath and combed my hair one last time.

Inside the bank, a lovely personal loan specialist—fresh out of college and on her way to grad school—assured me that Destiny and I had adequate equity in our house and sufficient credit scores to qualify for a sizable loan at a modest rate.

She never asked what we intended to do with the funds, and I never volunteered.

We're going to use fifty thousand to help find a three-year-old girl, and we'll spend another fifty or a hundred thousand to bail her mother out of jail and pay her legal fees.

The words seemed unreal residing in my head. I couldn't fathom bringing them out in the open, thereby giving them credence.

Brooke, the banker, gave me the loan application packet and told me that she looked forward to hearing from me soon. I mumbled something socially appropriate and fled before signing anything.

A quarter of a million dollars.

That was the sum Destiny and I had available to us. To borrow. To be forced to pay back, one agonizing month at a time, for years. From the deposits of a single income stream, if Destiny lost her job.

My armpits were drenched before I made it back to the car.

Would we go that far?

I sincerely hoped not.

On the way to the office, my thoughts of financial ruin were interrupted by a call from the police detective I'd met with the night before.

I shared his news with Fran as soon as I walked through the door.

"Detective Procaccio of the Denver Police Department called five minutes ago. He arrested Jasmine Smith at her home early this morning."

"That soon?" Fran lurched forward in her executive chair, almost hitting her stomach on the desk. "She put up a fuss?"

"She surrendered quietly. Apparently, another girl filed a complaint against her three months ago. The police had been building a case."

"Our evidence added to the pile?"

I nodded. "It helped. The detective thinks bond could be set as high as five hundred thousand dollars."

"That much?" Fran muttered, her face flush.

"She's considered a flight risk and a danger to her victims."

"Egad! We flippin' ruined her life!"

"Jasmine Smith ruined her own life," I said bluntly. "Also, the lives of at least four girls that we know about. Brittany Stallworth, Carly Siegel, Katie Mathers and the girl who filed the complaint. Jasmine didn't meet these girls by chance. She taught them, coached them and was supposed to protect them. She was in a position of trust. Are you listening to me?"

Fran mumbled something inaudible and refused to remove her hands from her ears or raise her head.

I spoke more loudly. "She did this repeatedly. Not one kiss, one mistake, one time. She had sex with underage girls hundreds of times, at least *four* different girls. What's the matter with you? You should be proud of the work we've done."

She lifted her head and shot me a furtive look. "Easy for you to say."

I let out an exasperated sigh. "What's going on, Fran? Why isn't it easy for you?"

"They wanted it. Every one of those girls asked for it."

"First of all, that's questionable. If you'd been here yesterday to interview Katie Mathers, you might feel differently. Second, even if they did consent, at their ages, it doesn't make a difference. According to the law—which was written for this reason—they were legally incapable of making their own decisions."

"Brittany Stallworth's almost seventeen," Fran said defiantly.

"Katie Mathers and Carly Siegel were fourteen when Jasmine Smith had sex with them. That's why she's facing felony charges. If she's found guilty, she'll go to prison for twenty-four years."

"Twenty-four years!" Fran croaked. "We did this to another lesbian? You and me did this?"

"Stop it! We didn't do anything. This woman is a sexual predator. Why is that so hard for you to accept?"

"Could be a mistake. Might be some error with the photos in Chelsey's camera. Brittany could be fibbing, trying to draw attention to herself. Girl seemed shifty both times I interviewed her." Fran's pace quickened. "Maybe the girls didn't like Jasmine. Made it all up."

"Jasmine Smith confessed," I said quietly.

Fran stared at me. "Forced admission. Police brutality. Happens all the time."

"Do you want to hear how the interrogation went?"

She shrugged. "What's it matter? Going to tell me anyway."

"When Detective Procaccio began the interview, Jasmine answered every question with, 'I don't recall.'"

"What I tell you? Innocent!"

"As he presented evidence, however," I said with care, "the case you and I helped build, she began to crack. At first, she claimed she thought the girls were eighteen."

"Carly and Katie were in eighth grade," Fran said faintly.

"Detective Procaccio played a tape for her, an incriminating conversation the complainant had recorded. After that, she wept and claimed she was embarrassed and ashamed."

"Emotions should have been used to prevent the relationships, not later excuse them," Fran said, sounding more like herself.

"Exactly!"

"Dang."

"Don't feel guilty about this. We did the job we were hired to do."

She shook her head back and forth in slow motion. "Never thought it'd turn out like this. Not in a hundred million years!"

"Jasmine Smith chose her prey among adolescent students and players and groomed them for sexual relationships. Those relationships were based on control and dominance."

Fran looked at me through half-closed eyes. "Not sex?"

"C'mon! She could have had sex with women her own age. Or with her husband."

"Not love?"

"Hardly."

Fran's head dropped to her chest, and she began to cry softly.

CHAPTER 25

In the span of an hour, I'd traded one set of tears for another. Fran Green's for Gwen Martin's.

Whereas Fran's had leaked out one at a time and dried up as soon as I tried to comfort her, Gwen's were falling in a steady stream down her splotchy cheeks.

My own eyes remained dry, incapable of filling, much less overflowing.

After I'd arrived in Highlands Ranch and relieved Destiny of her guardian duties—kissing her hello and good-bye on the front porch—I'd trudged into the house, only to find Gwen lying in the middle of the kitchen floor, naked.

I'd persuaded her to put on a robe and led her to the living room, where she curled up on the couch.

"I keep wishing this was a bad dream, wishing I would wake up and nothing would be real."

"I know."

"In the beginning, I had hope, although everyone told me I shouldn't. That's why I went out looking for Kayla every day."

"You had reason to hope."

"I'm not looking anymore. I was counting on a miracle . . ." Gwen's voice trailed off.

"It might not be too late. What about the woman at the bus stop, the one with the little girl who looked like Kayla?"

She shook her head. "The man who called in that tip was lying. He has a gambling problem, and he needs the reward money."

"Destiny gave you an update?"

"Lieutenant Longhorn called an hour ago."

"The lead about the woman in Littleton might pan out," I said supportively.

Gwen made a feeble attempt to sit up. "That was a waste. The woman's taking care of her niece. I wish I could see her again."

"Kayla?"

"Tracey. Just one more time. I wish I could take back all of the hurtful things I said on Tuesday."

"You both were under a lot of stress."

"I miss her so much. I don't know how I'll get through this alone." She paused for a hiccupping sob. "She was clean."

"I'm sure she was."

She pushed her hair away from her face. "The drug and alcohol tests came back negative. Destiny's police friend said that, too."

"That's good."

"I wish the Westminster police would tell the media, so people would stop trashing Tracey. All those mean people, saying nasty things about her. They don't know how beautiful she was. Only I do. And Kayla," Gwen said in a wail. "What's happened to my family? What did I do to deserve this?"

"You didn't—"

"Why am I being tortured? No one should have to experience anything this awful!"

"Gwen—"

"I have no reason to live. Everything I care about is gone. I should go to a pawn shop and get a gun—"

"You don't mean that. What if Kayla's still alive? She needs you. Leads are coming in every hour. All we need is one accurate tip, and we'll find her."

Gwen rubbed her eyes. "You don't believe that, do you?"

"I do. As soon as Fran gets here, I'm going to the Lesbian Community Center to review every tip line call again," I said, improvising. "I'll read each one ten times if I have to."

"Why? What's the point?"

My voice broke. "You can't give up."

"Honest and truly," Gwen said with fury. "No more bullshit. Look at me!" Her voice rose to a scream. "Look at me and tell me that my daughter's coming home."

"I can't," I whispered. "I wish I could."

"I didn't think so."

We stared at each other for a few rotten seconds, and then she buried her head in the couch pillows and began to sob again.

I sat motionless, feeling as if I'd just gone through a carwash without a car. I had no idea what to do next, but the doorbell provided a temporary answer.

"I don't want to see anyone," Gwen moaned as I rose.

I peeked through the curtains and let out a gasp. "It's your mom."

"Oh, God! Tell her to go away."

"Are you sure? I could—"

"No!" she said violently. "Get her away from me."

I slipped through the door and closed it with an inadvertent bang.

"Gwen's not receiving visitors right now," I said politely.

Dara Martin's plump hands were folded across her chest, and she stood stiffly. "Who are you?"

"Kristin Ashe. I'm a friend of Gwen's."

"Well, I'm Gwen's mother. Dara Martin."

"I recognize you from your television interview," I said, but didn't share that stretch pants, a flowery sweater, sturdy shoes and no make-up made her look older in person than she had via satellite.

"Let me in . . . please."

"I can't do that."

"I need to speak to my daughter."

Dara took a step toward me, and I backed up against the door. "I can pass along a message, if you'd like."

"How's she holding up?"

"She's managing."

"Is she shaking?"

"A little," I said, taken aback by Dara's insight.

"She used to shake like a leaf when she'd done something wrong. Is she taking care of herself? Eating well?"

"She's eating," I said simply.

"Gwen always did have a healthy appetite." Dara released a smarmy smile. "I won't stay but a minute."

"Not today."

The smile vanished, leaving behind pinched features. "She's not behaving the way a normal person would behave."

I folded my arms across my chest. "Why are you here?"

"I came to talk my daughter into turning herself in to the police."

"Excuse me?"

"My granddaughter deserves a proper burial."

"Gwen doesn't know where Kayla is."

"So she says."

"You don't believe her?"

"She always was mysterious. Sneaking around, keeping secrets."

"You haven't seen her in twelve years."

"Thirteen, but I know who she is, what she's capable of."

"You last saw Gwen when she was a teenager, yet you think you how her well enough to believe that she killed her child and hid the body?"

"Her or that other woman. Gwen knows more than she's letting on. I saw it in her face when she was on TV. She should do what's right."

"Tracey died last night."

"Who?"

"Gwen's partner. Tracey Reid. That other woman."

Dara raised an eyebrow and smirked. "That's for the best."

"The best?" I said heatedly.

"Gwen can stop covering for her and tell the truth, like I taught her."

"Do you have any compassion for your daughter?"

"How dare you judge me!"

"Do you have any interest in helping her?"

Dara Martin eyed me suspiciously. "I don't know what you're talking about."

"If the police come to arrest Gwen today, would you and your husband be willing to bail her out?"

"She needs to own up to what she's done."

"What if she's innocent?"

"Has she asked for our help?"

"No," I said grudgingly.

"Just as I thought. She's too good for us."

"Would you put up the money?" I persisted.

"How could we? We don't have the means. We're retired and living on a fixed income."

"You own two thousand acres in eastern Kansas," I said, using information Gwen had mentioned in passing in our first interview. "You could put up a portion of the land as collateral."

Dara shook her head stoutly. "We couldn't risk it."

"There wouldn't be any risk. Not unless Gwen didn't show up for her court dates."

"That land's meant to be passed on to our children, and to their children."

"Use Gwen's portion only," I suggested.

"There is no portion."

I glared at her. "You cut her out?"

"My daughter cut herself out when she decided to live a life without morals. What we do with the land is a family decision."

I stifled a sigh. "Could you talk to your husband?"

"I don't see what good it would do. My husband doesn't like to waste money."

"It wouldn't be wasted. You'd get back all of the money, except for a ten-percent fee that goes to the bondsman. I'm sure Gwen could pay you back over time. She has a good job."

"Does she?" Dara replied in a snippy tone. "She couldn't very well pay us back if she's sent to prison for life, could she?"

I looked over Dara's left shoulder, at the protestors who were clutching rosaries while they completed another Mass lap. "If I can get a commitment for the ten percent, would you be willing to put a lien on the land for the rest?"

"My daughter needs to take responsibility for who she is and what she's done."

"Yes or no?"

Dara hesitated. "I'll talk to my husband."

"Thank you," I said sincerely.

"But I can tell you what he'll say. He'll tell you that prison might give Gwen time to reflect on the choices she's made."

A few minutes later, Fran came bounding up the driveway. "That who I think it was?"

I nodded. "Gwen's mother."

Fran took another look at Dara Martin's backside, after which, she directed an arched eyebrow at me. "She and Gwen have a nice chat?"

"Gwen wouldn't let her in."

"Just as well. No time for a family reunion, not after your mum's trashed you on the boob tube." Fran hid her hands behind her back. "Pick a hand."

"Left."

"Wrong. Right." She thrust her right hand in front of me and waved a piece of paper. "Get a load of this."

I grabbed the sheet from her, and we sat in the wicker chairs on the porch. With Fran's eyes fixed on me, I read a five-paragraph summary of how Wren Priestly had financed her software business.

When I finished, I stared at Fran in amazement. "If this were to come out, no lesbian or gay organization would ever take money from the United Lesbian Foundation again."

Fran shrugged. "So be it."

"We'd risk that?"

"In a New York second. Who's our client?"

"Destiny?"

Fran made a popping sound. "Think again."

"Kayla Martin?"

"Righto! That's where our loyalties lie. You got the guts to follow through?"

"If I have to."

Fran tapped the crystal on her Mickey Mouse watch. "No time like the present, kiddo."

My eyes widened. "What am I supposed to do?"

"Showdown. Got an appointment for you."

"You did? How?"

She reached into her back pocket. "Don't ask. Won't have to tell. Here's a map."

"A map?" I said, slow to absorb this new strategy.

"To the Wren's mountain home."

"You want me to leave now, to do *your* dirty work?"

"Sooner better than later," Fran said with her most winsome smile.

CHAPTER 26

I steered past a parade of Christian protestors with one hand and dialed Destiny with the other, careful to keep my swerves limited to near misses, not outright collisions.

Destiny didn't answer her cell, which prompted me to ring the main line of the Lesbian Community Center. The receptionist put me on hold for eight minutes before Destiny cut in.

"Sorry. I was on the other line with Hillary. She just came out of a meeting with Seth Dunfey, the police chief."

"Does he feel guilty about Tracey's death?"

"Not at all. He's disappointed that he lost the possibility of turning one of the mothers against the other."

"Seriously?"

"Seriously. He's frustrated that he can't figure out which one's dominant."

"What difference would that make?"

"His theory is that the dominant one killed Kayla and hid the body on her own, or killed Kayla and forced the other one to help with the cover-up."

"He doesn't know what he's talking about. Gwen and Tracey are both innocent."

"You believe that?"

"I do."

"Obviously, Seth Dunfey doesn't. Yesterday, he spent most of the day working out details for a plea deal for Tracey, to get her to confess. He's convinced she was in possession of critical information. Now, he intends to come after Gwen."

"He thinks she's guilty?"

"He doesn't care. He just needs to save face. He plans to formally name Gwen as a suspect."

"Soon?"

"She could be arrested any minute."

Panic caught in my throat. "Hillary said that?"

"Not directly, but that's what she implied."

"Gwen won't survive in jail. Not in the state she's in."

"Is Fran with her?"

"Practically on top of her."

"Where are you?"

"In my car. I'm on my way to re-interview Bruce McCarthy," I lied.

I wasn't going to Bruce McCarthy's. Not to his home in Capitol Hill or to his Clock Tower office downtown.

Contrary to the lie I'd told Gwen, I wasn't on my way to the Lesbian Community Center either. I had no intention of wasting any more time on tip line leads.

Instead, I was headed to Idaho Springs, to confront the Lesbian Community Center's most generous supporter with unflattering facts from her past—a move Destiny never would have approved.

Destiny broke into my thoughts. "I forgot to ask earlier, how did it go at the bank?"

"Great," I said, adding to my pile of lies.

"Are we rich?"

"On paper."

"Did you fill out the paperwork for a loan?"

"Not yet."

"How much can we borrow?"

"A lot."

"Fifty thousand?"

I hesitated. "More like two hundred and fifty."

I heard Destiny's sharp intake of breath. "Should we do it?"

"Use it all?"

"Or as much as necessary?"

I gulped. "I guess."

"The first fifty thousand would replace Wren's reward money. How much will legal fees be if the police arrest Gwen?"

"I have no idea. You're the one who sent the lawyer."

"What about bond?"

"I don't know, Destiny. I've never done anything like this," I said, tensing.

"We still have the sixty thousand in donations that came in before the police press conference," she said, as if talking to herself. "That'll help. Contributors could ask for their money back, but so far none has. That gives us three hundred and ten thousand total."

"What if Gwen Martin's not innocent?"

"You just said that she was."

"That was before I knew I had to risk a quarter of a million dollars for a woman we met last week. Why do *we* have to do this?"

"Because," Destiny said calmly, "no one else will."

I wish I could have mirrored Destiny's placid nature, but I felt completely rattled by the time I reached the turnoff to Wren Priestly's home twenty-five miles west of Denver. For the last two miles, I bumped along dirt roads above Idaho Springs, eventually ending up on a remote lot in a dense forest of evergreens.

I parked my Honda on the cobblestone driveway and cut across the footbridge that led to the massive home that was built into a hillside of granite boulders.

At the ornate door, Wren greeted me warmly and insisted on giving me a tour of the twelve levels of the house, split across two floors. As she took care to point out the indoor lap pool and multiple balconies that overlooked the mountains and plains, all I could think about was the quarter-million Destiny wanted to risk.

In the cavernous great room, I declined Wren's drink offer, and once we were seated across from each other in oversized leather sofas, I handed her the report Fran had compiled.

While Wren read the damning synopsis, I gazed out floor-to-ceiling windows, to the snowcapped Continental Divide. "Does the end justify the means?" I commented casually, after she took off her reading glasses.

"The relevance of that question eludes me," she said in a cold tone.

"Fifteen years ago," I replied matter-of-factly, "you transferred money from the Atlanta Gay and Lesbian Chamber of Commerce into your own company, Priestly Enterprises."

She set her glasses on the table next to her. "I had to make payroll."

"That would be a yes? The end did justify the means?"

"I knew that if we could get to the next level of capitalization, we'd exceed investor expectations. I was not mistaken."

"You used money that didn't belong to you."

"I was working hundred-hour weeks. I did what was necessary to keep the doors open."

"You should have been arrested."

Her eyes flashed. "I started my company from scratch, with no backing. I grew Priestly Enterprises into a global powerhouse. We reached a thousand employees and a billion dollars in revenue. I've given tens of millions to the lesbian and gay community in the past ten years."

"Tell that to the lesbian in Atlanta who lost her coffee shop, or to the six dying men who had to find alternative housing when the AIDS hospice closed."

Wren crossed her legs and plucked at the crease in her pressed designer jeans. Between the jeans, the calf-length riding coat and pea-sized diamond earrings, Wren Priestly had spent fifty grand or more dressing herself. "I settled all prior claims," she said in a brittle voice.

"So what? By the time you paid back the two hundred thousand you'd leveraged into millions, it was too late."

"Other circumstances were in play at the time."

"Really?" I said in a friendly manner. "When you volunteered to be the executive director of the Atlanta chamber, did you plan from the start to comingle the chamber's funds with your own?"

"I resent your implication."

"Essentially, the chamber funded your business's growth. True or false?"

She looked me in the eye. "That's a distorted view of the facts."

"Improper use of organization funds. What would you call that?"

"That was never proven."

"Nonetheless, it's true, isn't it?"

"I had a vision that extended well beyond Atlanta."

"You drained all of the money out of the chamber's capital fund. Thirty years of community fundraising went into your pocket."

"I paid back those loans in full."

"You submitted invoices from Priestly Enterprises for services that were never rendered."

"The chamber board approved every expenditure."

"You kept money from an annual gala—door receipts and silent auction proceeds."

Her cheeks reddened. "People call me a visionary."

"You had checks from the chamber made out to a shell company that funneled the money into Priestly Enterprises."

"I couldn't have foreseen external market forces."

"You bankrupted the Atlanta chamber, and when it went under, so did an assortment of small businesses and organizations."

Wren folded her hands in her lap. "I was being pressured from every direction. I couldn't trust anyone."

"A bookstore and coffeehouse. A community center and theater. A hospice and newspaper."

"The bank called in our line of credit when financial markets tightened. Clients, investors, suppliers and creditors were on my back. I couldn't sleep. I couldn't eat. But I pulled through eventually."

"Good for you. Too bad the Atlanta lesbian and gay community never recovered."

"There were extenuating circumstances beyond my control."

"Are you trying to tell me you stole money because you couldn't *not*?"

"Don't take that tone with me."

"Tracey Reid smoked meth because she couldn't *not*. How are you two different?"

"I changed," Wren said nastily. "I turned my life around. I dedicated myself to philanthropy."

"What if Tracey changed, too?"

She shook her head. "That's not possible."

I leaned forward. "What if her second chance was ripped from her through no fault of her own? What if she were telling the truth about what happened to Kayla?"

Wren blanched. "That's ridiculous. If Tracey Reid were innocent, why would she have had a heart attack yesterday?"

"Because of the unrelenting pressure. Because no one believed her."

She waved dismissively. "Whether Tracey reformed is immaterial."

"Then why did you withdraw the fifty-thousand-dollar reward?"

"Because in the world of philanthropy, credibility means everything. Appearances trump reality."

I settled back into the sofa. "I agree. Which is why it would serve you to honor your commitment to Kayla and Gwen Martin."

"Can't you understand? I'm a change agent!"

I kept my tone even. "Then change your position on the reward. Double it, or every bit of information you see in that report will show up on the front page of the *Denver Post*. From that point forward, I assume, no reputable nonprofit will risk accepting funds from your foundation. Appearances trumping reality and all."

"You wouldn't dare!" Wren sputtered. "The impact on the community would be far-reaching and devastating."

"I know," I said in a defeated tone.

"Without my grants, twenty organizations in this city would close immediately, hundreds nationwide."

"Reinstate the reward."

"Political agendas that have been in the works for years would collapse overnight."

"A hundred thousand dollars," I said dully.

"Do you have any notion of what you're asking? You'll set gay and lesbian activism back fifty years, disrupting the lives of millions, the futures of every generation."

"I don't care about millions. Just one."

"I'm making investments in long-term change, initiating dialogue that will take place over decades."

I didn't blink. "Kayla Martin."

"My sole purpose is to strengthen lesbian and gay communities."

"Make the call or lose it all."

"Did Destiny send you to blackmail me into doing your bidding?"

"I came on my own."

"You're making a grave mistake," Wren said between clenched teeth. "Turning this into something personal."

"You made it personal when you abandoned Kayla and threatened Destiny. This is business. Put the reward back in place."

"Or?"

"Be prepared to face the same level of scrutiny Tracey Reid and Gwen Martin have faced for the past week."

CHAPTER 27

People had way too much time on their hands, and they were far too paranoid.

Those were the main conclusions I drew after five hours of studying calls that had come into the Kayla Martin tip line.

After leaving Wren Priestly's, a pang of conscience had driven me to the Lesbian Community Center, where I'd leafed through a dozen three-ring binders, searching for something I could bring back to Gwen.

Anything.

Fat chance of that, though.

Callers to the tip line had conspiracy theories ranging from UFO abductions to sexual slavery trades, and they suspected everyone. The people they lived near, worked with, made love to—no one eluded scrutiny.

Everything became a clue, from a pair of sneakers in a trash can to a mother carrying a duffel bag in a park. Black trash bags, in particular, took on ominous meaning, and little girls with blond hair and blue eyes were in peril on every street corner in Colorado, or so it seemed from the cascade of calls.

Wren Priestly's fifty-thousand-dollar reward had sparked a veritable treasure hunt, with interest and participation spiking after every morning, noon and evening newscast.

Unfortunately, there were few keen observers in the pack. In most reports, details were sketchy at best, absent at worst. Someone saw something, sometime, somewhere. Only a fraction of the leads had been copied and forwarded to the Highlands Ranch Police Department. Most of the rest should have been delivered to mental health professionals.

I wondered why Fran and I had gone to the trouble of blackmailing Wren.

Undoubtedly, someone knew something about Kayla Martin's disappearance.

In the end, however, I concluded that the person had yet to call the tip line.

On the way home from the Lesbian Community Center, to cheer myself up, I stopped by Taco Bell, a fast-food choice I hadn't exercised since high school.

For hours afterward, the Burrito Supreme sat in my belly like a molten brick while I relived segments of my afternoon conversation with Wren, congratulating myself on certain sentences, wishing aloud I could go back and edit others.

Around midnight, I finally dropped into bed, exhausted beyond compare, but sleep refused to come.

Eventually, I placed a call. "Destiny, are you awake?"

"What's wrong?" she said frantically.

"Nothing. I'm okay. Are you okay?"

"Honey, it's two in the morning. Why are you calling?"

"I don't know."

"You can't sleep?"

"No."

"Did you try lying upside down?"

"Twice."

"On the couch?"

"Once."

"You want to come here, to Gwen's?"

"No. I'd never get to sleep there."

"I could hold you," she whispered. "I could stroke your hair. Or other parts . . ."

"Destiny!"

"Sorry," she said, sounding anything but.

"I hate being in that house."

"I know."

"Everything reminds me of her. That little chair in the kitchen. The pink backpack on the coat rack. The puddings cups in the refrigerator. Can't they move that stuff? I can't breathe when I see it."

"I know."

"How do you do it?"

"I don't. I have to shut down before I turn onto Pine Lane, or I'd strangle a Christian on my way up the driveway and fall apart the second I stepped foot in the house. I haven't even noticed most of the stuff you mentioned. I can't."

"That can't be healthy, shutting down all the time."

"I'm coping, Kris. I'm trying to help a good person get through a horrible time. Every time I feel myself losing it, I think how much worse I'd feel if I were Gwen."

"When this is all over, can we take a nice vacation? Somewhere safe and peaceful, where awful things never happen?"

"Where would that be?"

"Inn at the Governors in Santa Fe."

Destiny laughed lightly. "We'll go away for a long weekend as soon as this is resolved, I promise."

"I don't know what I'd do if anything happened to you."

"Nothing's going to happen to me."

"You don't know that. You get death threats every week. You drive like a maniac. You have a history of heart disease in your family."

"Kris, Kris, Kris."

"I couldn't—" I halted.

"Kris!"

I fought back tears. "What?"

"I'll love you for the rest of our lives."

"But we don't know how much rest we have."

"Enough," Destiny said in a soft tone. "We'll have enough."

"Ever tell you about my summers away at Camp Winnipeg?" Fran called out six hours later, mere minutes before eight o'clock, though it felt like five o'clock.

The damp, gray weather had only exacerbated my sleep-deprived condition. "No."

"Best times of my life, Catholic camp," Fran said, a deadness in her tone. "Five glorious summers in a row, ages nine to thirteen. Gorgeous acreage. Up near Aspen, off Highway Eighty-five. Fabulous weeks."

I took my seat next to her in our office, lowering myself as if every joint in my body needed oiling. "What's brought on this wave of nostalgia?"

"Easier times back then. Fishing holes and swimming ponds. Weenie roasts and cowboy cookouts. Starlit nights and meteor showers. Canoe rides and tire swings."

"Fran—"

"Never a dull moment. Horseshoes. Archery. Tennis. Horseback riding. But that ain't what stands out the most."

"What? Did you meet your first girlfriend at Catholic camp?"

"Indubitably." Fran blushed. "Landed my first kiss, too. Summer of my thirteenth year. On the bottom bunk in a log cabin, during an afternoon thunderstorm. Locked lips and thought I'd died and gone to heaven."

"What was her name?"

Fran rubbed her chin. "Sherry McKee. Angelic face, strong hands, hair down to her hips. First awakening. First love. First heartache."

"At thirteen," I said, keeping my tone even. "You were precocious."

Fran cracked a smile. "Always was mature for my age, and sped up even more after the hormones caught fire. Heavy-duty flirting, both sides, gave way to kissing. That led to sessions of groping and fondling. Started above the belly-button, but moved south in short order."

I put up a hand. "Okay. Okay."

"Eventually full-blown sex. Nude, one-hundred-percent body contact. Couldn't get enough of her, sweet Sher. Craved her. Had to sit near her. Listen to her. Smell her. Touch her. She lit up all my senses. Prettiest one in camp."

"Prettiest camper?" I said carefully.

Fran averted her gaze. "Counselor."

I took a deep breath. "Sherry was a nun?"

"Layperson, employed by the camp . . ." she said, her voice fading.

"How old was she?"

"Thirty-six."

I remained expressionless. "How long did it last?"

"Just the one month of that summer."

"Did you know what you were doing was wrong?"

Fran rubbed her cheeks. "Not at the time. Too caught up in the excitement. Couldn't quite reconcile the girl-on-girl action, but never gave the age difference much thought."

"Sherry must have."

"Agreed, or she wouldn't have told me to keep quiet. You know me, big blabbermouth. Can't keep the trap shut when I'm fired up about something. Acted shame-filled, Sher did, now that I look back. Told me our friendship was different. Had to keep it on the Q-tee. Fine by me, long as I could keep touching her."

I shifted uncomfortably. "I'm so sorry, Fran."

She waved. "Don't be. Agreeable, I was. Went along willingly. Sometimes was the instigator. Nothing forced on me. Made my own choices."

"You couldn't have given consent."

"Certainly did," she said, attempting a lecherous grin. "Time and again."

"You were too young," I felt like yelling, but instead said in a low voice, "That's why it's against the law."

"Different times back then. Wasn't talked about. No sex offender designations. Never heard of anyone facing felony charges."

"That degree of intimacy, at that age, with that much of an age difference—it must have disrupted your life."

"People make mistakes."

"It sounds like Sherry groomed you."

Fran's eyes moistened. "Felt affection for her. Still do."

"She was supposed to set the boundaries."

"Chased her like a stalker, I did. Made sure I got into her group activities. Sneaked around camp, pretended to bump into her."

"That's typical teenage behavior. You didn't cross a line. She did."

"Wasn't a troubled teen. Not me. No, siree. Just smitten. Head-over-heels with my first crush. Thoroughly enjoyed it. Kept coming back for more. Got no right to complain."

"Fran!"

"Not a victim," she continued stubbornly. "Never have been. Never will be."

"Did you ever tell anyone about what happened?"

Fran shook her head. "Nope."

"You never talked about it?"

"Not a word. Zipped lips till today."

"Do you wish you had?"

"Have lately. Been giving it a lot of thought, ever since Brittany 'fessed up about Jasmine. Ever since you and me been beating this topic to death all week. Different names, same experience. Been wondering if it damaged me."

"I don't know how it couldn't have."

Fran's forehead wrinkled. "Secret drove a wedge in my life, that's for sure. Between me and my mum. Me and my friends. Me and my everyday life. Lost interest in my favorite activities. Got behind in my schoolwork after camp ended. Started me down a rocky road. Looking back, can see how Sher crept into my life and stole a piece of me."

"That's understandable."

"At camp, felt like the relationship was divine. Don't get me wrong. Felt hot, too," she said with a forced laugh. "Knew I was sinning, though. No question there. Kept coming back to the love. That much love, couldn't be wrong."

I cleared my throat. "Fran—"

"Really regret not talking to my mum, though," she said in a stronger voice. "We shared everything."

"You didn't feel like you could?"

"Not at thirteen."

"Or later?"

"Nah. Would've broken my mum's heart, made her feel like a failure. Should've told someone, though."

"You didn't feel like you could confide in anyone at the camp?"

"No, and don't go bad-mouthing the church. Catholic church made me who I am. Good and bad. Ain't going to throw stones at the institution."

"I won't say anything about the church. We don't have enough time."

She cracked a smile at my humor. "Appreciate that."

"How long did Sherry work at the camp?"

"Only the one summer, far as I know. Shook hands when we parted, front of my mum's Olds. Last time we touched."

"You didn't go back to camp?"

"Tried the next summer. But when Sher wasn't there, felt heartsick. Asked my mum to come get me." Fran put her hand over her mouth and shook her head. "Nothing simple about this. Not fifty-some years ago, when it happened. Not in the last week, when the memories came crashing back to life."

"You could have talked to me."

"Doing it now. Doing the best I can," Fran said, rising and walking toward the door.

CHAPTER 28

Fran returned in less than five minutes, breathing heavily. She ran both hands through her gray crew cut. "You in the mood for steak and kidney pie?"

"Fran!"

"Sorry about the high-tail. Had to clear my head. Power-walked around the block. Feel much better."

I studied her with concern. "Are you okay?"

"Better than before. Confession's good for the soul."

"Do you want to talk some more?"

"Not now. Not about me and Sher, but appreciate the shoulder to cry on."

"Anytime."

"Back to work. How about bangers 'n mash? Too early for a pint, but might get a good cup of tea."

"What are you talking about?"

"Take a wild guess who drives a monkey-shoe car?"

"How can I guess when I don't even know what that is?"

"Mini Cooper. Red with white stripes."

"Ah," I said, at last. "To a nine-year-old girl, that's a car that looks like a shoe on a cartoon monkey. Marla Semper?"

Fran's face fell. "How'd you know?"

"That's who you were supposed to be checking out. Tracey's meth friend."

"Check I did." She handed me a pink Post-it. "Traced the car through motor vehicle registration. Got the rest through a social security trace."

"What's a Gastropub?" I said, uncertain whether I was reading her note correctly.

"Modern British-style pub in northwest Denver. Neighborhood hangout off Thirty-Second Avenue. Ate there once. Had indigestion for days. Brit bites bit me. Had to buy new undies, if you catch my drift."

"Too much information." I winced. "Marla Semper works there?"

"Morning shifts. Ought to skedaddle. Get to Marla before the cops twist her and the facts."

"They haven't interviewed Marla?"

"Once, according to Destiny. Placed a wake-up call to your sleeping beauty at the stroke of six this a.m. Destiny imparted info she got from Detective Hillary. The men in blue took a shot at Marla day before yesterday. Grilled her about the storage locker she shared with Tracey. Never connected her with the scene of the crime on the day Kayla vanished."

"We're the only ones who know about this? That Sierra Frazier saw Marla's car in front of the house on Thursday afternoon?"

"Don't know a thing. Speculation only," Fran said disingenuously. "Monkey-shoe, Mini Cooper. Wouldn't exactly call that withholding vital evidence. Not till we confirm."

"We tell no one?"

"Nary a soul."

"Not even Destiny?"

"Especially not her. Destiny gives us up to Hillary, and those yokels she works with'll bungle everything. Our lead, our first crack."

"All right," I said with reluctance. "But we can't sit on this too long if it proves promising."

Fran grinned. "Wouldn't dream of it."

"What are you going to do this morning?"

"Comfort Gwen. Keep the Christians at bay. The usual."

I grabbed my car keys. "I'll come by the house when I'm done with Marla."

"You do that. Now get going! Got a good feeling about this."

I didn't have a good feeling.

Not about anything.

Not about what had happened to Fran when she was a teen.

Not about what might have happened to Kayla on Thursday, September 13.

My mood improved slightly, however, with a call from Destiny. "Guess what? Wren reactivated the reward."

"Really?"

"She doubled the amount. She's putting up a hundred thousand."

"Wow?" I said, grimacing when the word came out sounding even more forced than my previous comment.

A long pause followed. "Did you talk to Wren? You didn't, did you?" Destiny groaned. "Tell me you didn't."

"Briefly. Yesterday afternoon."

"Oh, no! What did you say?"

"Not much."

"What made her change her mind?" Another pause. "I don't want to know, do I?"

"I wouldn't, if I were you."

"Will you tell me someday?"

"Maybe. But not until we're very, very old."

"We're growing old together?"

"Not anytime soon."

Destiny laughed. "I have more good news."

"Good. I could use some."

"After he was released from prison, Todd Robie molested two children in Highlands Ranch."

"How exactly does that qualify as good news?"

"Maybe not good news, but it makes me feel less guilty about his death."

"How did you find out about the other kids?"

"Hillary called. The parents came forward after they saw news reports about Robie's murder."

"Did Hillary say why they haven't arrested Gwen yet?"

"She doesn't know. They've cut her out of the meetings."

"Her personally?"

"An entire group of officers has been reassigned."

"How's Gwen doing this morning?"

"Not well. I was up with her most of the night."

"Doing what?"

"Listening to her cry. Trying to convince her that Kayla's still alive. Telling her not to worry about Tracey's funeral arrangements. Or being arrested. It was a long night," Destiny said wearily. "I'll be glad when this is over. Are you coming down here this morning, or is Fran?"

"Fran should be there any minute."

"What're you doing today?"

"Right now, I'm following up on a lead."

"What is it?" Destiny said excitedly.

"I can't tell you."

"Kris!"

"I promised I wouldn't. As soon as I know something for certain, I'll call you. Don't say a word to Gwen."

"I won't."

"I mean it, Destiny. Don't get her hopes up again."

"Oh, no," she said, her voice fading. "You think Kayla's dead, don't you?"

"I don't think anything," I hedged. "I'm just following a lead."

The moment I saw the red and white Mini Cooper parked in front of the Gastropub, I felt uneasy.

I had a sinking feeling I was about to interview a kidnapper or a murderer.

I wanted to believe Marla Semper was a kidnapper, and that Kayla was stashed somewhere, unharmed, but in the back of my mind, I knew better.

Three waitresses were flitting about in the crowded restaurant, and I sensed immediately that Marla was the one with the black wig and pasty complexion.

Marla's face clouded when I explained my reason for stopping by during a work shift, but she agreed to take a short break. She led us to a table in the corner of the restaurant, near the bathroom, and we sat below a Union Jack draped across the wall.

The space looked less like the dark, intimate English pub I'd imagined and more like a former coffeehouse, reconfigured with framed British posters spread across white walls. Concrete floors and tin ceilings accentuated the din to an uncomfortable level, and I had to lean in to catch Marla's words.

"I feel bad about what happened to Tracey."

"Her death?"

"That, too."

"What did you mean?"

"Her little girl. The reporters going after her. The police blaming her for my shit."

"You're talking about the identity theft supplies in the storage unit?"

Marla nodded. "A long time ago, Tracey rented a unit for her shit, and she told me I could put my shit in it. She never messed with my crap, and I never messed with hers."

"Never?"

Marla blinked rapidly, which riveted my attention to her heavy blue eye shadow and Sharpie pen eyebrows. "Maybe I looked through her boxes once or twice, but I never took anything. She didn't have anything good. Just old photos and knick-knacks. Shit like that."

"When did Tracey stop using the storage space?"

"After she came out of rehab. She took her shit out and told me we couldn't be friends anymore."

"Why?"

"Because I was using every day."

"How did you and Tracey meet?"

"Friend of a friend," she said vaguely.

"Did you give Tracey a free sample of meth?"

"Maybe," she said vaguely.

"When did you start forging checks?"

Marla leaned across the two-top. "Six months after I got hooked on meth. I needed money for my habit. I was using five hundred to a thousand dollars of crystal a month, and I kept getting fired from jobs. One day, I sat down and came up with a list of choices. Give up the drug. No way would I do that. Whore out. I'd tried that once. Never again." She ticked off the options on her slender fingers. "Cook meth. No, thank you! I'd been to cooking parties. You know what goes into making meth? Striker strips from boxes of matches. Sudafed. At parties, you sit around and tear strikers and punch out tablets. Add drain cleaner and lithium from car batteries, yummy," she said sarcastically. "Knowing me, I would have blown myself up on my first batch. But when I was a kid, I'd always been good at drawing, and I loved calligraphy. Forging checks seemed like a good plan."

"Did you do a lot of it?"

Marla sat back, put her hands behind her head and smiled slyly. "Way more than anyone knows. My checks were golden. I'd stay up for three, four days straight, tinkering away. Then I'd crash for two days. I made payroll checks for me and other tweakers, and we cashed them at grocery stores. I stole purses from chicks at bars and got their credit cards and bank information. It was a cool game."

"Was Tracey involved?"

"Never."

"What made you stop?"

"The meth or the checks?"

"Both."

"I stopped the shit with checks when I stopped using."

"What made you get off meth?" I prompted after it seemed as if Marla had lost her train of thought.

"One night, my boyfriend, in this shit-brained drug binge, beat me over the head with a lamp. The day after I got out of the hospital, I was arrested for possession. It's all worked out for the best, but it sucked at the time."

"You went to prison?"

"Fuck, no!" she said with a slight smile that exposed ill-fitting dentures. "The judge sentenced me to rehab, four years of probation, random drug testing, the whole deal. It's a pain, but the program and the supervision keep me straight."

"The police questioned you last week because you never took Tracey's name off the storage unit?"

"My bad." Marla shrugged. "I never thought about it, to tell you the truth."

"When did they contact you?"

"Tuesday."

"How did they find you?"

"The manager at the U-Rent place gave them a copy of one of my checks. A real check. I'm all legit now."

"Did you admit to the police that the ID theft supplies belonged to you?"

Marla rolled her eyes. "No, or they would have sent me to prison for violating the terms of my probation."

"So you accused Tracey?"

"I'm not a narc. I told them I didn't know anything about anything."

"You didn't tell the police that you'd been to Tracey's house on

Thursday?"

"Fuck no! With my history, they would have automatically thought I was guilty. No one trusts tweakers."

"Should they?" I said, no inflection in my tone.

"Not usually, but this time, it wasn't me. I didn't touch that little kid."

"Just out of curiosity, what made you get back in touch with Tracey?"

"My sister-in-law lives in Highlands Ranch, and she ran into Tracey at the pool over the summer. She told me all about Tracey's girlfriend and kid. I decided to look her up. I wanted to apologize."

"For what?"

"For getting her hooked. Narc-Anon shit."

"What time did you come by Thursday?"

"Morning."

"Early morning? Late morning?"

"I'm not really good with time," she said, shrugging.

"Did you stay long?"

"Not when I knew I wasn't welcome."

"Tracey wasn't happy to see you?"

"You could say that." Marla smiled uncertainly. "She was sick with her cold and all."

"Did you meet Kayla?"

"Sure. She was on the porch, holding onto Tracey's leg. Cute kid, but I scared her, maybe. I have that effect on kids sometimes."

"You didn't go inside the house?"

She shook her head. "Tracey wouldn't let me, but I was cool with that. Never trust a meth head. Once a druggie, always a druggie."

"How long have you been clean?"

She squinted. "Three months and two days."

"So you came by on Thursday to apologize to Tracey, not for any other reason?"

Marla stared at the table. "Amends. One of the steps in the program."

"Not because you needed money?"

"I always need money, but Tracey offered. I didn't ask."

"How much did she give you?"

"Two hundred."

"You left after you got the money?"

"She made me. She didn't want me interfering with her routine."

"You never came back?"

"No."

"That's strange," I said deliberately, "because an eyewitness saw your car in front of the house Thursday afternoon."

Her breaths became more shallow. "I didn't do nothing."

"But you did go back?"

Her eyes darted back and forth. "Maybe."

"When?"

She put two fingers to her mouth and started chewing on the nails. "Three or three thirty. Something like that."

"To get more money?"

"Maybe. But Tracey didn't answer the door, so I left."

I gazed at her intently. "You expect me to believe that?"

Marla shrugged. "Ask the chick next door. She saw me."

I stiffened. "Which chick? Which side?"

"The house with the glider on the porch. To the west, no south. Whichever. Ask her. She was on her way to the gym."

To the south. Kim Frazier. My heart started pounding wildly. "How do you know where she was going?"

Marla frowned. "She was carrying a gym bag."

I kept my tone even. "What did the bag look like?"

"I don't know. It was white, with a blue, circle-type thing on it. One of those karate logos."

"What did the woman do with the bag?"

"She put it in the back seat of her station wagon, I think. I wasn't really paying attention. Why?" Before I could answer, Marla's face turned ashen. "You don't think . . ."

Yes, I did.

I did think that Kim Frazier had been carrying Kayla Martin's body.

CHAPTER 29

I waited five excruciating hours for Sierra Frazier to come home from school.

When she did, she wouldn't answer any of my questions, not until she'd changed into her white martial arts uniform and shown me a sequence of punches and lunges. Each Tae Kwon Do move set the pink ball on her ponytail band spinning, and I grew more impatient with every demonstration.

After she completed her routine, she stomped her foot, bowed and sat on her bare heels.

I dropped to the ground next to her, on the lawn between her house and Kayla's, and crossed my legs underneath me.

I couldn't take my eyes off the flying foot logo on her uniform. "Can we play the hot-cold game?"

"You want to hide something," Sierra said excitedly. "Candy? Or a bracelet? I love bracelets."

"No," I said, drawing out the word.

"I get to hide something? What should I hide?"

"This is a different version of the game. We play in our minds. I ask questions about something that happened, in real life, and you tell me if I'm hot or cold."

"Oh," she replied in a small voice.

"Want to play?"

A look of apprehension crossed her eyes. "Do we have to?"

"Only for a few minutes. It's really easy. Watch! Last Thursday, the day Kayla got lost, you went to school. Am I hot or cold?"

"Hot."

"After school, someone came to visit you."

"Hot."

"A boy."

"Cold. Freezing cold," she said, warming up to the spirit of the game.

"A girl."

"Hot."

"The lady in the monkey-shoe car."

"Cold."

"Kayla."

"Hot!" Sierra blurted out before covering her mouth.

"It's okay," I said gently. "I can understand why you were afraid to tell anyone. You invited Kayla to your house to play."

She fiddled with the end of her brown belt. "Cold."

"You went into Kayla's bedroom while her mom was sleeping and asked her to come over."

"Cold."

"Kayla walked over on her own."

"Hot."

"To your house."

"Warm."

"To your tree house," I amended.

"Hot."

"She brought something with her."

"Hot."

"Her Garfield."

"Hot," Sierra said, the look on her face a cross between a smile and a frown.

"And the two of you played together."

"Hot."

"Dolls."

"Cold."

"Stories."

"Cold. I'll give you a hint," Sierra whispered eagerly. "Something I love."

"Tae Kwon Do."

She clapped her hands together. "Hot!"

I kept my tone nonchalant. "Something happened."

"It wasn't my fault," she said, her eyes widening. "I'll get in trouble with Master Lee when he finds out."

"Finds out what?"

"That I don't have my bag. He says we're supposed to treat our worldly belongings with care."

"How did you lose your bag?"

"I didn't lose it. Mommy took it. She told me to go to my room and not to leave. Not for any reason. She was really mad."

"Did she take Garfield, too?"

"Yes," Sierra mumbled.

And later planted it on the median of Highlands Parkway, for volunteer searchers to find on Sunday. "Was Mommy mad about what happened in the tree house?"

Sierra nodded glumly. "Kind of."

I put my hand on her knee. "Where you practicing one of your kicks?"

"Mmm, hmm," she groaned.

"Kayla moved when she shouldn't have, and you hurt her?"

Sierra made a face. "Not on purpose."

"Did Kayla cry?"

"She didn't make any noise," Sierra said in a rush. "She just fell down. I tried to make her get up, but she wouldn't. She turned all blue, and she couldn't close her eyes. I told her I was sorry, but she wouldn't say anything. Why wouldn't she say anything? Is Kayla coming home?"

"No."

"Where is she? Can I see her?"

"I'm afraid not."

"Mommy said I could see her again. In heaven," Sierra wailed. "Mommy promised."

"When did she tell you that?"

"When she closed Kayla's eyes and put her in my bag."

CHAPTER 30

For the first time in a week, I no longer felt a sense of life-or-death urgency.

Death was the answer, and with it came a slowing down of time.

Leaving Sierra's playhouse, I knew what I had to do, and I set about the task with a plodding determination.

At any juncture, I could have called the police. Or Destiny. Or Fran.

But I didn't.

I wanted to be the hero. As if there were some heroism in bringing back the decaying body of a child, to the only parent who had survived the ordeal of her disappearance.

On the afternoon that Kayla went missing, a dog walker had seen a woman in "corporate clothing" sitting in a car at the Plum Creek trailhead in Chatfield State Park. On the tip she'd called in to the

Lesbian Community Center three days after Kayla vanished, the dog walker hadn't included the make or model of the vehicle. She had, however, noted the insignia of a foot on the white gym bag in the back seat of Kim Frazier's car.

I'd read the tip at least twice, but hadn't understood its gravity until I combined it with details from Sierra's confession.

In less than ten minutes, I drove from Highlands Ranch to the entrance to Chatfield, where I parked next to the southern fork of Plum Creek trail.

For the next several hours, in precise sweeps, I circled back and forth, across miles of paths and grasslands.

Lightning threatened in the distance, and rain blurred my vision, but I continued until I was almost delirious with despair.

Finally, in the span between dusk and darkness, I spotted a suspicious mound of dirt, no more than 200 yards off one of the main paths. I ran to it and began to frantically dig. Fighting through sobs that wracked my body, I pulled a white gym bag from the soil and clutched it tightly to my chest.

I knew I was disturbing evidence, perhaps destroying it, but I didn't care.

All that mattered was Kayla.

That at last, she could come home.

Publications from Spinsters Ink

P.O. Box 242
Midway, Florida 32343
Phone: 800-301-6860
www.spinstersink.com

ACROSS TIME by Linda Kay Silva. If you believe in soul mates, if you know you've had a past life, then join Jessie in the first of a series of adventures that takes her *Across Time*. ISBN 978-1883523-91-6 $14.95

SELECTIVE MEMORY by Jennifer L. Jordan. A Kristin Ashe Mystery. A classical pianist, who is experiencing profound memory loss after a near-fatal accident, hires private investigator Kristin Ashe to reconstruct her life in the months leading up to the crash.
ISBN 978-1-883523-88-6 $14.95

HARD TIMES by Blayne Cooper. Together, Kellie and Lorna navigate through an oppressive, hidden world where lines between right and wrong blur, sexual passion is forbidden but explosive, and love is the biggest risk of all. ISBN 978-1-883523-90-9 $14.95

THE KIND OF GIRL I AM by Julia Watts. Spanning decades, *The Kind of Girl I Am* humorously depicts an extraordinary woman's experiences of triumph, heartbreak, friendship and forbidden love.
ISBN 978-1-883523-89-3 $14.95

PIPER'S SOMEDAY by Ruth Perkinson. It seemed as though life couldn't get any worse for feisty, young Piper Leigh Cliff and her three-legged dog, Someday. ISBN 978-1-883523-87-9 $14.95

MERMAID by Michelene Esposito. When May unearths a box in her missing sister's closet she is taken on a journey through her mother's past that leads her not only to Kate but to the choices and compromises, emptiness and fullness, the beauty and jagged pain of love that all women must face. ISBN 978-1-883523-85-5 $14.95

ASSISTED LIVING by Sheila Ortiz-Taylor. Violet March, an eighty-two-year-old resident of Casa de los Sueños, finally has the opportunity to put years of mystery reading to practical use. One by one her comrades, the Bingos, are dying. Is this natural attrition, or is there a sinister plot afoot? ISBN 978-1-883523-84-2 $14.95

NIGHT DIVING by Michelene Esposito. *Night Diving* is both a young woman's coming-out story and a thirty-something coming-of-age journey that proves you can go home again. ISBN 978-1-883523-52-7 $14.95

FURTHEST FROM THE GATE by Ann Roberts. *Furthest from the Gate* is a humorous chronicle of a woman's coming of age, her complicated relationship with her mother and the responsibilities to family that last a lifetime. ISBN 978-1-883523-81-7 $14.95

EYES OF GRAY by Dani O'Connor. Grayson Thomas was the typical college senior with typical friends, a typical job and typical insecurities about her future. One Sunday morning, Gray's life became a little less typical, she saw a man clad in black, and started doubting her own sanity. ISBN 978-1-883523-82-4 $14.95

ORDINARY FURIES by Linda Morgenstein. Tired of hiding, exhausted by her grief after her husband's death, Alexis Pope plunges into the refreshingly frantic world of restaurant resort cooking and dining in the funky chic town of Guerneville, California. ISBN 978-1-883523-83-1 $14.95

A POEM FOR WHAT'S HER NAME by Dani O'Connor. Professor Dani O'Connor had pretty much resigned herself to the fact that there was no such thing as a complete woman. Then out of nowhere, along comes a woman who blows Dani's theory right out of the water.
ISBN 1-883523-78-8 $14.95

WOMEN'S STUDIES by Julia Watts. With humor and heart, *Women's Studies* follows one school year in the lives of three young women and shows that in college, one's extracurricular activities are often much more educational than what goes on in the classroom.
ISBN 1-883523-75-3 $14.95

DISORDERLY ATTACHMENTS by Jennifer L. Jordan. The fifth Kristin Ashe Mystery. Kris investigates whether a mansion someone wants to convert into condos is haunted. ISBN 1-883523-74-5 $14.95

VERA'S STILL POINT by Ruth Perkinson. Vera is reminded of exactly what it is that she has been missing in life. ISBN 1-883523-73-7 $14.95

OUTRAGEOUS by Sheila Ortiz-Taylor. Arden Benbow, a motorcycle-riding, lesbian Latina poet from LA is hired to teach poetry in a small liberal arts college in Northwest Florida. ISBN 1-883523-72-9 $14.95

UNBREAKABLE by Blayne Cooper. The bonds of love and friendship can be as strong as steel. But are they unbreakable?
ISBN 1-883523-76-1 $14.95

ALL BETS OFF by Jaime Clevenger. Bette Lawrence is about to find out how hard life can be for someone of low society standing in the 1900s.
ISBN 1-883523-71-0 $14.95

UNBEARABLE LOSSES by Jennifer L. Jordan. The fourth Kristin Ashe Mystery. Two elderly sisters have hired Kris to discover who is pilfering from their award-winning holiday display. ISBN 1-883523-68-0 $14.95

EXISTING SOLUTIONS by Jennifer L. Jordan. The second Kristin Ashe Mystery. When Kris is hired to find an activist's biological father, things get complicated when she finds herself falling for her client.

ISBN 1-883523-69-9 $14.95

A SAFE PLACE TO SLEEP by Jennifer L. Jordan. The first Kristin Ashe Mystery. Kris is approached by well-known lesbian Destiny Greaves with an unusual request. One that will lead Kris to hunt for her own missing childhood pieces.

ISBN 1-883523-70-2 $14.95